Robert G. Bar... ...worked mainly ... ...moved to Terriga... ...w South Wales. Robert has ... ...ber of films and TV commercials bu... ...concentrate on a career as a writer. He is the author of *You Wouldn't Be Dead for Quids*, *The Real Thing*, *The Boys from Binjiwunyawunya*, *The Godson*, *Between the Devlin and the Deep Blue Seas*, *Davo's Little Something*, *White Shoes, White Lines and Blackie*, *And De Fun Don't Done* and *Mele Kalikimaka Mr Walker*.

THE DAY OF THE
GECKO

ROBERT G. BARRETT

PAN
Pan Macmillan Australia

As usual, the author is donating a percentage of his royalties to Greenpeace.

First published 1995 in Pan by Pan Macmillan Australia Pty Limited
St Martins Tower, 31 Market Street, Sydney

National Library of Australia
cataloguing-in-publication data:

Barrett, Robert G.
The day of the gecko.

ISBN 0 330 35722 0 (pbk.).

I. Title.

A823.3

Typeset in 11/13.5pt Times by Post Typesetters, Brisbane
Printed in Australia by McPherson's Printing Group

*This book is dedicated to my English teacher at Randwick Boys' High School, Mr William (Bill) Neeson, for the odd clip across the ear, boot in the backside and those wonderful, warm words at the Bondi Beach Public School reunion, when I proudly gave him two autographed copies of my books —
'Barrett, you were the biggest ratbag in the class. And you were the only one that learned anything.'
Thanks, Bill.*

A MESSAGE FROM THE AUTHOR

After ten years of writing Les Norton stories, and a lot of enquiries, I feel it's time I cleared up a couple of things for my loyal and loveable readers. Firstly, a lot of people are wondering why the last two Les Norton books were set overseas. Am I now turning into some millionaire, jet-setting, Harold Robbins type of author, Concorde-ing round the world? Florida, Jamaica, Hawaii one minute. Next it'll be Paris, Rome, London, Zurich. The only reason I set two books overseas was because I knew people there. I knew a bloke in Florida and I do have an Aussie mate who's a cop in Honolulu. The Jamaican thing happened because I wanted to visit Cinnamon Hill Great House, the ancestral home of Elizabeth Barrett Browning. While I was there I thought I'd write a Les Norton story. As for me being a millionaire — hah! Though I have met some in my travels. But the majority I've met haven't impressed me all that much. So basically I just go where I think I can get a story. And as I'm not real keen on travelling out of Australia, you can expect plenty of stories set here from now on. But going by the letters and by talking to my readers, I think Les should go over to England at some stage and see how his mate Perigrine is getting on.

Secondly, I'm also getting heaps of readers asking me if there is a Les Norton fan club? The answer is a definite NO! I don't like the term 'fan club'. Madonna and Kylie Minogue have fan clubs. So do Take That and Rod Stewart. I like to think I have *readers*. And a good team of readers at that. So we came up with an idea — Team Norton T-shirts. I took a few with me on my last book tour and they tore the last one off my back outside the hotel in Cairns. Initially, we were going to distribute them through bookshops. But that way any mug can walk in off the street and buy one. Therefore we have decided to keep them exclusively for my readers. So here's what the deal is. You get a choice of four white T-shirts. On the front in full colour is the cover of either YOU WOULDN'T BE DEAD FOR QUIDS, THE BOYS FROM BINJIWUNYAWUNYA, MELE KALIKIMAKA MR WALKER or THE DAY OF THE GECKO. Printed across the back is TEAM NORTON. Send a cheque for $32, along with your size (M, L, XL), choice of T-shirt and address it to Psycho Possum Productions, PO Box 3348, Tamarama, Sydney NSW, 2026. We'll cover the postage. Remember though — these T-shirts look absolutely sensational and they're for Les Norton readers only. So if any mugs ask where you got them, don't tell them, or they'll all want one. But just think of it — you walk into a pub or a club or whatever, wearing your TEAM NORTON T-shirt and you spot someone else wearing one. You've got an instant mate. You're part of a team — Team Norton.

Thanks for giving me ten years of enjoyment. I'll see you in the next book.

Robert G. Barrett
August 1995

Nestled in the very corner of North Bondi, where Ramsgate Avenue begins its climb towards Ben Buckler, is a small cafe and take-away food business called Speedo's. It's about two doors up from North Bondi RSL and set on one side of two buildings — a private hotel and a small block of apartments. Two black awnings, split in the middle by a blue and white sign saying Speedo's, have SPEEDO'S CAFE in white painted on one and TAKE AWAY painted neatly on the other. Above the two signs, the brown wooden tiles of the hotel balconies cling to the stucco concrete face of the private hotel as they climb towards the roof. Floor-to-ceiling glass doors face the street, there's a blackboard out front which says coffee, juices, salad, focaccias, etc, and beneath the glass doors, built at an angle onto the footpath to allow for the rise of Ramsgate Avenue, are two long, narrow wooden tables and stools. A sign shaped like a world globe on the cafe door says SPEEDO'S CAFE TO THE WORLD and inside are more stools, counters, chairs and tables lorded over by a large red coffee machine. Small framed posters hang on the walls, there's a full blackboard menu and the ubiquitous coffee shop notice-board with small ads for writers' workshops, aromatherapy, skin care, therapeutic ryoho yoga, etc, etc. The take-away side just has a refrigerated drinks cabinet, the take-away menu, another coffee machine and whatever. For its size, Speedo's does a thriving business because the food is good and the coffee is arguably the best in Bondi, which isn't a bad rap because restaurants and coffee shops are just about cheek-by-jowl now all over Australia's most famous beach.

The view from Speedo's on a good day isn't too bad either and, on this particular Monday morning in early February at around 10.00 a.m., it could have been a little better, but it wasn't too bad at all. Although the ocean is partially blocked by a row of spindly, scrubby trees running alongside the park and a faded pine log fence that meanders up Ramsgate Avenue, you could still see North Bondi Surf Club, the pink outline of the Bondi Hotel, some of the waves and the white sand running all the way beside the promenade to the skateboard ramp and the brittle, green grass of the park at the south end. Despite a brisk rather cool southerly blowing, there was a cluster of people with their towels, radios and things on the sand outside North Bondi Surf Club, joggers on the wet sand and other regulars either slogging it out on the soft sand or doing exercises or stretches at the exercise station in the park alongside North Bondi Surf Club. Amidst all this were the power walkers striding along the promenade, arms flailing as they flung their hand-weights either up and down or side to side as they marched along either to a

Walkman or their own particular cadence. Waxheads were few and far between. As well as the southerly blowing, it was low tide, so what small waves there were were getting dumped onto the sandbanks into choppy, shapeless white foam. Now and again a beach inspector in his blue uniform would zoom up on a beach buggy, take a look around, then do a U-turn and zoom back off in the direction he came. It was a mild sort of a morning for a summer's day in early February. Some puffy, grey clouds hung around and over the horizon, buffeted gently along by the southerly, and above these was another layer of clouds going in a different direction, so thin they looked like they'd been smeared across the sky. Somewhere in the middle, part of the moon still hung in the sky, a small, fading white crescent against the blue.

So all in all, apart from the wind and the few clouds around, it wasn't a bad sort of summer's day and the view from Speedo's was pretty good. However, from the point of view of the thick-set, red-headed gentleman in the Levi shorts and white T-shirt seated on the wooden stool closest to the beach, as he stared out over his cup of coffee next to an empty bottle of orange Gatorade, the view was pretty bloody lousy. In fact, for all he cared about the weather and the view, it could have been pissing down rain while he gazed into the murky, stagnant water of an abandoned quarry. Once more, Les Norton's cup of happiness had turned into a rusty tin mug full of dried leaves. And once more it was Warren's bloody fault. Les had been kicked out of his own home; Chez Norton's in Cox Avenue. The boot. Out. Piss off and don't bother coming back.

3

Though to say he'd been kicked out was a bit of an exaggeration and Les did manufacture things in his mind at times. It was more of a voluntary exile. Whatever it was, Norton didn't like it. And it was definitely Warren's fault.

The trip back from Hawaii had been fairly uneventful. Les never quite let on he knew Warren had been porking a TV celebrity's young daughter-in-law and, if Warren suspected Les knew, he never mentioned it. Les cashed Andrea's cheque, Warren's burns healed up and he went back to work and life went on pretty much as before at Chez Norton's. A few nights a week at the Kelly Club, which was split with Billy Dunne, so it could have hardly have been easier. And when they did work, all they had to do was keep an eye on Price and his mates while they played cards, mainly Manilla, on credit, munched nibblies, drank piss and cracked jokes. You had to be a member now to get into the club, so there was no drama much to speak of at the door and Les was getting to meet some very interesting people at times. It was almost as much fun going to work now as it was going out or staying home, plus he got paid for it; and when it was quiet, if they didn't get away early, Les could sit around and read a book or a magazine. Apart from that, it was get some exercise, go swimming or sit around the beach and have a perv on the beautiful girls. Les had rung DD a couple of times and was even thinking of going up and paying her a visit. So all up, life and times were pretty good at Chez Norton's. Then, one night at a bar in Bondi, Warren met Isola; a skinny, six-foot-two-inch Dutch backpacker with brown hair, brown eyes, white teeth and a homely, if unsmiling, sort of face.

4

Warren had brought her back to the house three days before and Isola, along with her backpack, had been there ever since. The only saving grace was that she was pissing off to Indonesia with one of her Euro-trash, backpacker friends on Saturday. Not that Les minded Warren having a girl in the house; plenty of girls had stayed there at different times. But virtually from the minute Warren walked in the door with Isola, all they did was root. They didn't make love, they didn't fornicate, they didn't screw. You could say they fucked. But mainly what they did was root. At first, Les found it rather amusing because he didn't think Warren had it in him. But Warren was making up for lost time and he was also making every post a winner. They rooted in Warren's bedroom, they rooted in the hallway, they rooted in the bathroom and they rooted in the kitchen. Les wasn't at all surprised when he walked into the laundry one day with his smelly gym gear and there they were, going for it like a pair of sea-soned-up hyenas, underneath the clothes dryer.

Les wasn't quite sure if they'd ripped one off on his bed, though he had his suspicions. But he didn't mind all that much. And Les didn't mind if they started root-ing in front of him while they were watching a video in the lounge room or if Isola would start giving Warren a head job while he was trying to watch the news. Les didn't mind either if he walked out in the backyard and Warren would be giving Isola's ted a giant munch on a blanket next to the toolshed. It wasn't as if Warren was trying to impress Les with all the bonking; he and Isola were just two young, hot arses deeply in lust and they were going for it. Warren had even taken a week off work to be with her and it was good to see his flatmate having the time of his life.

What Les did mind, though, was being treated like a stranger in his own home. In fact it was worse than that. It was almost as if Norton didn't even exist or he was invisible. Les realised poor Warren was completely pussy-whipped and could see nothing except Isola's brown map of Tasmania. But Isola completely ignored Les. She didn't speak to him, she didn't look at him, she somehow didn't even seem to acknowledge Norton's very existence. It was weird; and Les somehow minded that. But what Les did mind was one morning when he walked into the kitchen to find another stack of dirty dishes, cups, pots, pans, knives and forks, and just about anything in the kitchen you could possibly get dirty, overflowing out of the sink, across the greasy stove and dripping down into a bulging kitchen tidy that was being steadily strafed by several fat blowflies that were probably bursting with maggots. Norton wasn't at all looking forward to cleaning this horrible mess up, when Isola walked in wearing a pair of saggy blue knickers with half her grumble hanging out, no make-up, hair all over her head and smelling both of BO and some sheila that had spent the night rooting. As usual, she completely ignored Les while she found a clean glass and poured herself a drink of water.

'Hello, Isola,' said Les, trying his best to sound friendly. There was no answer. Then Les casually remarked, 'I wish you liked cleaning up as much as you like rooting, Isola.'

Isola took a sip of water and without looking at Les

said, 'If you don't like, why you don't fuck off.' Then she walked back into Warren's bedroom and closed the door.

That had been earlier this morning. Since then, Les had left the mess in the kitchen, jogged six laps of Bondi on the soft sand, paddled four on the surf-ski, did a particularly mean thirty minutes on the heavy bag at North Bondi Surf Club, where he'd showered and changed; now he was seated outside Speedo's staring morosely across his coffee cup and wondering what sort of sentence a magistrate would give him if he belted a certain Dutch backpacker right on the chin. Apart from that cop in Florida, Les had never hit a woman and didn't think a great deal of men who deliberately did. But Isola was in dire need of a short right under the lug; leaving shit all over his house, then telling him if he didn't like the idea he could fuck off was definitely making the cup of tea a little too strong. Maybe a year in the nick might be worth it? Get away from the whole scene for a while. Les shook his head. No, the legal fees'd be murder and she could end up suing me. Norton's eyes narrowed. Maybe I could electrocute the moll? Drop a hair dryer in the bath when they're both in there going for it after they surface around eleven. Get rid of both of them. No. I'd probably miss Warren when he gets his shit back together again. Plus the little prick owes me three weeks' rent. Les shook his head again. No. There was only one thing to do. Move out. Anywhere. Fuck it, it was only till Saturday. He glanced up at the private hotel above Speedo's. What about in here? Nice and handy to the beach. Or what about five nights up at the Ramada?

Give myself a spoil. Then Norton scowled. Yeah, that'd be right. One hundred and fifty dollars a night because I let some soapy backpacker kick me out of my own house. Les didn't know what to do. One thing he did know. If he went home, found all that shit was still in the kitchen and Isola gobbed off at him again, he was a special to tell her to get well and truly fucked herself, then kick her skinny Dutch arse out the door, along with her backpack, and Warren too if he didn't like the idea. Norton finished his coffee and was brooding about something he wasn't particularly looking forward to when he heard a woman's voice just to his right.

'Well, well, well, if it isn't Priscilla, queen of the gambling dens. What's the matter, darling? Somebody nick your handbag when you went to the ladies' room last night?'

Norton glanced up absently at an attractive woman around thirty wearing a maroon tracksuit and Reeboks, her dark hair held back in a tight ponytail. Perspiration glistened on her face from behind a white sweatband and dark sunglasses; a pair of light weights dangled at her side from two dainty hands. Les peered at the dark sunglasses for a second, then his face slowly broke into a smile; definitely the first one that morning.

'Side Valve Susie. Well, I'll be stuffed. And just as cheeky as ever. How have you been, mate?'

'Not too bad. Working mainly, trying to get in front. What about yourself?'

'Pretty much the same. Trying to keep the wolf from the door. To tell you the truth, I've just finished training. I got down here earlier.' Les glanced at Susie's tracksuit and the two weights. 'What are you up to?'

'I've just been for a power walk round to Bronte and back.'

'Shit! That's not a bad hike for a young city girl on her own.'

'Yeah, I did it a bit bloody tough this morning, too.' Susie puffed her lips and blew a couple of drops of sweat from the tip of her nose.

Les nodded. 'Yes, I think there has to be a better way than this.'

'Tell me about it. My feet feel like lead.'

'Well, why don't you plonk your sweet little backside down here and I'll shout you a bottle of Gatorade?'

Susie seemed to think for a moment as another drop of sweat formed on her nose. 'Yeah. I think that might be a good idea. I feel buggered.'

Les got up to let Susie in. 'Orange?'

Susie seemed to think for another moment. 'Lemon-lime.'

'Coming right up.' There were a few people in the take-away side so, while he was waiting, Norton reflected on how he got to meet Side Valve Susie.

It wasn't long after Les finished with Easts. He met her at a party in Rose Bay. They went out, got on famously, and even managed to get into each other's pants on a couple of occasions when they were consumed by the demon alcohol. They bumped each other in a hotel one night where Les was in an argument with two old Easts officials he was unlucky enough to come across. Susie put her head in, half-drunk, and started needling Les. Les was a bit testy and sort of told her to piss off. For which Norton copped what was left of

Susie's Bacardi and Coke over his head and she left with another bloke. Les bumped her again in the street and apologised for what he said, though he didn't feel like a drink tossed over him was needed. Susie sort of apologised too. She was a bit drunk. But the bloke she left with turned out to be not such a bad chap and had plenty of money. So see you round, Les, anyway, and no hard feelings. And that was that. No hard feelings. Les would see Susie now and again and Susie would always give Les a bit of cheek and they'd laugh and share a joke.

Susie's cheek, however, got Side Valve her comeuppance and her nickname one night at The Bridge Hotel in Balmain, listening to a band. Susie kept pitching up to this bloke she fancied, even though his girlfriend was there. As the girlfriend got drunker, she got shittier and ended up belting Susie on the chin with a roll of ten cent coins, breaking Susie's jaw. It wasn't all that bad, but somehow it took ages to knit and every time Susie spoke it came out the side of her mouth with a lisp a bit like Sylvester the cat. Some horrible, low, insensitive, sexist men at the North Bondi started calling her Side Valve Susie. And it stuck; amongst a few callous women too. Even today, Susie's jaw caught occasionally and she lisped the odd word now and again. Somehow, after that, Susie stopped going after other women's men and throwing drinks over blokes as well.

Les returned with the two Gatorades and sat back down alongside Susie. She thanked him, then they both took a drink. Susie had taken off her sunglasses to wipe her face and, despite a sweaty red face and no make-up, Les couldn't help but notice Susie still had those attractive Joan Collins type of features and when he bumped her getting up from the stool he noticed there was nothing wrong with her body. Side Valve Susie was still very much a good sort.

'Oh yeah. Good one, mate.' Susie belched politely into her hand. 'Thanks again, Les.'

'My pleasure, Susie.' Les took another swallow, then looked at her for a moment. 'So what are you doing with yourself now, Susie? I haven't seen you around for a while. Still hairdressing?'

'Yeah, casual. That and some waitressing. Plus I do a bit of buying and selling on the side. I bought a home unit, Les, and it's a constant battle between myself and the bank as to whether I should still be allowed to live there.'

'Yeah, I know what you mean. They can be drop-kicks all right. I'm lucky. I own my joint.'

'I got a young student staying with me at the moment. That helps a bit.'

Norton's eyes narrowed for a second. 'Yeah, I've got a boarder at my place too.'

'Warren?'

'That's him.' Les decided to change the subject. 'So what's this buying and selling you do? Guns, drugs?'

'That's more in your line, isn't it? No. CDs. Imports mainly. What about you, Les? What are you up to these days? You look good.'

'So do you, Susie. Don't worry about that.'

'Thank you, Les.'

Norton told her pretty much the truth. Casual work at the club. He'd had a couple of trips away. A bit of what happened. They laughed and joked. Susie said it was work mostly for her, trying to pay off a home unit. She hadn't been going out much and when she did it was generally no great turn-on *and* expensive. Les smiled at her and thought, 'why not?'

'Well, I get a night off from the pickle factory now and again. How about we go out and have a nice meal? Or see a movie? Anything you like. Just for old times' sake. This time, throw something over me I like. Jim Beam or Eumundi Lager.'

Susie tossed back her head and laughed, then put her hand on Norton's and looked at him. 'All right, Les. That sounds good to me. I always had fun when we went out together.'

Norton gave Susie's hand a warm squeeze. 'Did we ever.'

'The thing is, though, I'm flying down to Melbourne at seven tonight. I won't be back till Sunday.'

Les seemed to sense something in Susie's voice. 'Everything's okay? Nothing . . .?'

'Actually it's an old aunty died. She left the family two houses. So after the funeral and the weeping and wailing there's the reading of the will. And I'm not sure, but I think I'm in the whack. Shit! I hope so.'

'Yeah, wouldn't that be handy,' agreed Norton.

'So I'm away for a week.' Susie took her hand away and looked evenly at Norton for a moment. 'Les, would you mind if I asked you a small favour?'

'I suppose not,' shrugged Les. 'What is it?'

'Your place is only just round the corner from my unit. Would you keep an eye on it for me while I'm away?'

'What about the boarder? What's wrong with him?'

'He's away somewhere.' Susie's voice seemed to soften. 'It's two minutes from your place. I've got all this stuff there, and there's been some strange goings-on lately. For an old friend, Les?' she added with a coy smile that could have meant anything.

Norton stared at Susie. It was as if the heavens had opened up and all the storm clouds had rolled away, leaving great shafts of sunshine. The answer to his problem. Les looked briefly at the sky. You're up there, pal. I know you are.

'I'll go one better than that, Susie,' he said. 'How would you like me to move into the place while you're away? Guard it night and day. I'll do it for you, Susie.'

'You will?' Susie gave a bit of a double blink.

Les looked Susie straight in the eye. 'I've just had my place done over for white ants and Bondi butter-flies. The place is full of poisonous, deadly chemical smells. Plus I've had a carpet mob in.'

'Yes. It wouldn't be a bad idea to clean your place up, Les. The last time I was there, the dog next door used to leave its backyard to bury bones in your carpet.'

'Don't slag Chez Norton to me, tart. It's a palace. But I'll do that for you if you want, Susie, while my place is off tap.'

Susie looked at Les then gave him a quick cuddle and a peck on the cheek. 'That'd be great, Les. Thanks a lot.'

'Any time I can help. You know me.'

'I sure do.' Susie winked and raised her bottle. 'Well, come on, let's finish these and I'll show you where I live. I have to start making tracks anyway.'

'Okey doke.' They finished their drinks and began walking towards Campbell Parade. Les offered to carry Susie's hand-weights in his bag. Susie accepted.

Les lived barely five minutes from the beach and, with parking and all that, it was easier to walk down, and even better if you found someone nice to walk back with. They nattered on about nothing much at first. How Bondi with its myriad trendy restaurants and coffee shops was now the new Hollywood Babylon and everybody you met was either an actor or a writer, or a film producer or a director. Some were. But there was no shortage of wannabes and gunnabes either. They also agreed Bondi was a nice place through the week, but if you were a local you just stayed inside and locked your doors on the weekend. Les and Susie couldn't split what they liked about the weekend circus the best. All the roid-heads who'd been doing three-tonne bench presses, strutting round in their lycra shorts and cut-away singlets. Or the Western suburbs wogs, in or out of work, screaming around in the gridlock with their car boom-boxes blasting out house music. Or maybe the suits on their Harley-Davidsons. Work in the bank or sell insurance all week, then come Sunday and stick the bandanna and vest on and it's rolling thunder up and down Campbell Parade. That was in the daytime. At night the complete rats and monsters took over the freak show. Good old Bondi. But it was nice through the week. The sushi and coffee were good and there was always the chance you might get discovered. Shit! Jason Donovan lived there and Kylie Minogue had a boyfriend there. That had to mean something. Les tried to pump Susie for a bit more SP about the boarder in case he should suddenly arrive when Les was there. His name was Ackerly and she didn't know where he was. He was a student writing a book on a grant. He rang up after two days, but before Susie could understand what he was talking about he hung up again. He'd only been there a couple of months, was very quiet and didn't say much; just seemed to be thinking all the time. The funny things that had been going on? Well, Susie just had this feeling her unit had been broken into. Nothing was missing. But Susie had this feeling someone had been in the flat. Maybe a perv. And the old Russian couple above her had moved out suddenly. It was only temporary she'd found out, but they both seemed agitated when they left as if they didn't want to go. Another two Russians had moved into their unit. A young bloke and an older one. The older one was always friendly and sort of joking, but there was something off-putting, even slightly sinister about them. Between them and all the other comings and goings and carryings-on around the units, Susie was grateful Les would be there while she was away.

The unit was about two hundred metres on the left-hand side of Hall Street, just past all the shops at Six Ways and pretty much like Susie said: just round the corner from Norton's house. Twelve brown brick units, trimmed with white concrete, faced the street and each unit had two cream-coloured brick sundecks; a long narrow one and a shorter, deeper one. Most sundecks were filled with pot plants and vines and there was a well-kept garden and lawn out the front. A driveway ran down the left to the parking area and a row of poplars separated Susie's units from a bigger block

15

next door. Susie's unit was on the bottom right-hand side. She had pot plants on her long, narrow verandah, which was next to the entry pathway, and some vine-covered latticework on the corner to stop people reaching over or getting onto the balcony too easily. She also had the name of the units painted in a scroll on her wall. Golda Court. It looked like a nice part of Bondi with lots of tall, leafy trees, wide grassy median strips, grand old homes and expensive-looking home units.

'Not bad, Susie,' smiled Les. 'Looks like you've done well, mate.'

'Yeah, I think so,' nodded Susie. 'Once I get in front it'll be better. Come down the back and I'll show you where the garages are before we go inside.'

'Righto.'

Susie led Les along a gravel path that went past her unit and the front door of the flats, to where there were more units and a door built out on the right. She opened it and Les followed her down an angled flight of stairs to the parking bay. There were twelve garages with metal roller-doors; Susie's was open all the time because the lock had jammed and empty because her car was in for repair. Another larger roller-door opened onto the driveway and worked by a buzzer; Susie said she'd give Les her buzzer when they went upstairs. She showed Les the garbage bay and where he could wash his car if he wanted to. Les had a bit of a look around, then followed Susie back the way they came. She opened the front door, a set of stairs ran up to the left, a hallway banked off to the left again past the other three ground floor units; Susie's was the one on the end. The key clicked in the deadlock and they were inside.

The unit was roomy, yet compact, with a decent-sized lounge room. A mirror wall next to the alcove as you entered and another at the end of a short hallway past the two bedrooms also added an illusion of size. A sliding door led to the kitchen and laundry on your left as you walked in and a sliding glass door led from the lounge onto the deeper of the two balconies. The lounge room edged in a bit next to the balcony which was where Susie had the TV. There was a bedroom door that was closed, another one half-closed along a short hallway with the bathroom opposite, and that was about it. The carpet was plain brown with matching cream wallpaper and curtains, and there were low-hanging soft light fittings. One of those solid wooden Spanish-style lounges and lounge chairs in red and yellow with matching foot stools and coffee tables ran along one wall. Framed posters hung on the walls, mainly old Marx Brothers movies or old rock stars: Buddy Holly, Janis Joplin, James Brown, Little Richard, though there was one of Prince or whatever he called himself now, with his new, odd-looking guitar. Plants and vines either sat or hung in the corners giving the place a little warmth and an obvious woman's touch. The best thing though — along the wall next to the kitchen and facing the lounge — was a stereo, the speakers separated by a table packed with hundreds and hundreds of CDs just like in a record shop. Beneath the table were boxes crammed with more CDs. Norton had never seen so many CDs in one person's home.

'Not a bad place you've got, Susie,' said Les, giving a nod of grudging approval. 'Modern, clean, roomy.

Like I said outside, you've done well. Good luck to you.'

'Yeah. Thanks, Les,' smiled the new owner. 'I . . . rather like it myself.'

Norton ran his eyes around the stereo again. 'I'll tell you what. Jesus! You've got some bloody CDs.'

'Yeah. Some of them I keep, but mostly I wheel and deal. I got a bloke gets me imports and I offload them to specialty shops and recycled record shops. There's a good earn there. You like music, Les?'

'Reckon.' Norton flicked through a couple of rows of CDs. 'I might tape a couple of these while I'm here — if that's okay?'

'Sure, go for your life. But you can see why I was worried about leaving the flat empty. I got a security alarm but if they got in they'd have all those out in two minutes. I can't claim insurance, because, to be honest, Les, most of them aren't quite kosher and the ones in my collection are irreplaceable.'

'Yeah,' replied Les absently, still looking at all the CDs like a kid in a toyshop.

'Anyway,' Susie started loosening her tracksuit, 'I'm going to have a shower. Make yourself a cup of coffee if you want. There's juices and cold water in the fridge.'

'Okay, thanks.'

Susie went into her bedroom and locked the door. Les soon heard the sound of a shower running and figured she must have an en suite in her room. He gave the CDs another loving look, then decided to make himself a cup of coffee.

The kitchen was all matching brown and white tiles

and brown-timber laminate and was a little wider than Les had first thought. It looked onto the pathway through a grilled window and a curtain. Cupboards ran round the walls and beneath the stainless steel sink set under the window. There were plenty of electric do-dads, a solid electric stove and a microwave oven. A large refrigerator hummed against the wall next to a breakfast table near the laundry door. A Mexican hat and a framed photo of some Mexican food and the recipe hung above the kitchen table.

Norton had no trouble finding what he was looking for and before long had the kettle boiled and a cup of instant in his hand, which he'd flavoured up with some Carnation he got from Susie's well-stocked fridge. Yes, this might just suit me, thought Les, as he sipped his coffee in the kitchen. I can do plenty of cooking here. Use all her food, it'll only go off. Try all sorts of things. Though I'd better not make too much mess. Shit! She keeps it clean. But what about those fuckin' CDs. Les moved into the lounge and slowly looked over the table full of CDs while he sipped his coffee. He'd never heard of half of them. Ronnie Earl and the Broadcasters. Shane Pacey and the Cigars. John Heartsman. The Leon Thomas Blues Bank. The Nighthawks. There was Zydeco. Rockin' Sydney. Terrence Simien and the Mallet Playboys. Country and Western. Confederate Railroad. Neal McCoy. The Kentucky Head Hunters. Shit! How good's this, thought Les. There's gotta be some top tracks amongst all this. He clicked his fingers. That's what I'll do as soon as I finish this coffee and get the keys, buy a stack of blank tapes and start going for it. Though I should offer poor Susie a lift to the airport. I'll do it first thing after.

Gaping at the CDs, Les didn't hear the shower stop and didn't hear Susie come out of her bedroom. She was wearing a long, loose, blue-striped Grandpa shirt, open a little at the front to give a glimpse of dainty white bra, and looking and smelling good.

'I see you managed to make yourself a cup of coffee. I hope you made one for me?'

Les smiled over to her. 'Susie, I knew you'd come out of that shower all freshened up and looking for either a stink or an argument. So I did. There's a cup ready to go near the kettle.'

'Oh! You're . . .'

'But don't move. I'll get it. Two sugars?'

'One.'

Les poured Susie a cup of coffee, handed it to her in the lounge room and had another look around.

'Yep. This isn't a bad set-up you've got here, Susie. I like the photo of Little Richard.'

'Yeah, it's coming together slowly but surely. It's just the bloody payments.' Susie put her coffee down on one of the small tables. 'Before I forget, I'd better show you how everything works.'

Susie showed Les how to work the stereo, the TV, the video and the intercom. She gave him the buzzer for the garage and a set of keys, also mentioning he may as well eat whatever was in the fridge as it would only spoil while she was away. She then led him over to the door.

'Now, Les, this is the security system.' Next to the door was a plastic box of small square buttons numbered one to ten with three tiny lights: red, amber and green. The amber one was on. 'Now the security number for the alarm is 1002. But so you don't get confused, you think of the movie *2001: A Space Odyssey*. Reverse it, which is 1002, and press it and that's it.'

Les looked at the box of numbers then looked at Susie. 'Let me get this straight. When I come in, I think of *2001: A Space Odyssey*. The movie?'

'That's right.'

'And I press 2001.'

'No. You press 1002.'

'But the movie's 2001.'

'Yeah. That's the movie. *Space Odyssey*.'

'2001.'

'That's right, Les.'

'So the security number's 2001.'

'No, Les. 1002. You reverse it.'

'Reverse the movie?'

'No! Not the fuckin' movie, Les. The number. 2001 is 1002. You reverse it.'

'Reverse it?'

'Yes, Les! You bloody reverse it!'

Norton looked at Susie, looked at the box of numbers, then looked at Susie again. 'But why?'

'So you don't get fuckin' confused, you moron.'

Norton shook his head. 'You've got me confused, Susie. And I've seen *2001: A Space Odyssey* about four times.'

'Oh, for Christ's bloody sake!'

'Susie. Just one more time and slowly. What's the number?'

Susie's eyes narrowed. 'Two thousand and fucking one is the movie. *Space Odyssey*. 1002 is the fucking security number.'

'The security number is 1002? Forget the movie.'

'That's right, Les,' breathed Susie. '1002.'

Les looked at Susie, completely devoid of expression. 'Well, why didn't you say so in the first place?'

Susie seemed to go a little funny. 'Les,' she said slowly, 'why don't we finish our coffee on the lounge. I think I've shown you all I can for now.'

'Okay.'

They put their coffees back down on one of the tables and sat on the lounge with Susie on Norton's left. She was shaking her head slowly and seemed to be staring at the floor as if she was trying to avoid eye contact with Les.

'You know what your trouble is, Susie?' said Les quietly.

'What!'

'Tension and stress. You're that uptight, Susie, it'd take a tractor to pull a thermometer out of your blurter.'

'You'd make . . .'

'It's all this work you're doing,' cut in Les. 'Hairdressing, waitressing, rorting CDs. The bank manager pounding on your door. You don't know where your boarder is. The break-in. Plus a death in the family. It all catches up, you know.'

Susie gave a little sigh. 'Yeah, you could be right, Les. I have had a lot on my mind.' She moved up the lounge a little closer to Les. 'It's not all peaches and cream for a single girl trying to survive in the city.'

'And Uncle Les understands.' He put his arm around

Susie's shoulder and she rested her head on his. 'You know what you need?'

'No, Les. What do I need?'

'A nice rub. Just round your neck and shoulders. Get rid of all that stress and tension. Before the rivets in your boiler pop.'

'You think so, Les?'

'I know so. I can see so.'

Susie let out a little breath. 'Yes, you could be right.'

'Well, why don't you sit down on the floor in front of me and I'll give your neck a rub.' Susie looked at Les. 'Take five minutes. Then I'll give you a lift out to the airport later. Save you catching a cab.'

'Would you?'

Les nodded.

'Oh, that'd be great.'

'Now, do you want a rub?'

'Okay. Why not?'

Susie took a cushion from the lounge and sat on the floor with her back and shoulders between Norton's knees. Les rubbed his hands together for a moment, then got gently to work.

Susie did have a few tiny knots in the nape of her neck and her shoulders were a bit tender, but her skin was smooth and lightly tanned with just enough muscle tone to make Norton's job interesting. He worked his fingers in softly but with just enough pressure to break up any little lumps and bumps that might have been troubling her. Before long, Susie was crooning and sighing and moving her head in tune with Norton's gently probing fingers. He held her head with his left hand and did the right side of her neck and held her

23

head with his right hand and did the left side of her neck, at the same time managing to massage her scalp and both her shoulders.

'Ohh, boy, that feels good,' she crooned.

'I told you,' said Les. 'I'll have those evil spirits and tensions out of you before you know it.'

'Mmmhhh, will you ever.'

Les rubbed and squeezed, then ran his thumb up and down Susie's spine through her shirt. 'Do you want me to do your back while I'm here?'

'Okay,' replied Susie, then she stood up. 'Wait till I get some oil.'

Susie went to the bathroom and returned with a bottle of baby oil. She handed it to Les, then took off her shirt, let it fall to the floor and stood in front of him for a moment in a pair of blue lacy knickers and a white bra. Norton swallowed hard and several beads of sweat formed on his forehead. Les rubbed some baby oil on his hands then sprinkled a few drops on Susie's back and away he went again, rubbing and caressing, moving his big hands clockwise then anti-clockwise.

'Ohh, Les. That feels unbelievable.'

'That's . . . good,' panted Les, glad that Susie had moved forward or she would have been leaning back against Norton's pounding third leg.

Les poured more oil on his hands, then ran the heel of his palm up and down Susie's spine with long, even strokes. Susie sighed out loud. With a quick, easy motion Les unhooked her bra and let it fall to the floor also. He ran his hands over her back and shoulders some more, then moved her to him and ran his hands around her nice firm stomach and two lovely, firm

24

little boobs. They felt delightful, the oil made them shine and in no time Norton's massaging had the nipples sticking up like two tiny, pink jelly beans. Susie's stomach started to heave and her breath seemed to tighten. She twisted on her side a little and looked dreamily, if not slightly angrily, up at Norton.

'God, you're a bastard, Les,' she said.

'Me?' Norton looked surprised. 'Why? What have I done?'

'You know what you've done.'

Les shrugged. 'Buggered if I know. I'm just trying to be nice.'

'Yeah, nice. You despicable, low shit!'

They looked at each other for a moment then Les bent forward and kissed Susie right on her luscious soft, red lips. She returned Les's kiss avidly and snaked her arms around his neck. They kept kissing. Susie's tongue came out as Les kept softly massaging her stomach and boobs with one hand and the nape of her neck with the other. Their kissing got hotter and hotter till it almost started to sizzle. Les ran his hand down over Susie's ted and found it just starting to get soft and moist beneath the lacy blue knickers. She opened her legs for a while and Les kissed and stroked, then stood up and grabbed Norton by the hand.

'Come on,' she said.

'Come on? Where?' asked Norton innocently.

'Ohh, where do you bloody think, Les. You arse-hole.'

Norton shook his head. 'Funny way to talk to an old friend who's trying to help you,' he said as he stood up and let Susie lead him into her bedroom.

As she shut the door behind them, Susie looked directly at Les. 'You haven't got any creepy crawlies or been hanging around with any low molls or old poofs lately have you, Les?'

'Not me,' assured Norton. 'I'm a heterosexual Christian and disease-free. Just ask my doctor or the local vicar.'

'Good! Because it's been a long time between drinks for me. And right now I've got the rhythm, so let's go.'

'God bless you, Susie. You're a better friend than I thought.'

By the time Les had his clothes off, Susie's blue knickers had vanished and she was lying back on the bed, legs apart, knees up a little and a pillow under her head. Norton climbed over her, ran his lips and tongue over her boobs and stomach, kissed her neck then her eyes and lips, all the time his knob resting about a centimetre from her lovely little, well-trimmed ted. Susie squealed and kissed Les hungrily as he ran Mr Wobbly around and in between her legs for a moment. Susie began to wiggle her backside around and by now her breathing was starting to sound like she was making cappuccino. Les kissed her a couple more times, raised his backside and slipped Mr Wobbly about halfway in; Susie gasped and went cross-eyed. Les stroked a couple of times then raised his backside again and buried the lot.

Susie choked off a scream and now it was Norton's turn to go cross-eyed; he started pumping away as chills ran up and down his spine. As Susie wiggled and squealed underneath him, she kicked her legs up in the air and kissed Norton's neck and lips. Norton could scarcely believe how tight and sweet Susie was; he groaned inwardly as Susie thrust herself up at him and hoped he wouldn't explode too early. Christ! To think blokes go to gaol for this, sell drugs, rob banks, commit murders, start fights, lose houses, ruin their lives. Susie kicked up again, Les caught her knees in the crooks of his arms, lifted her legs up over her head and sank in a bit harder and deeper. Jesus! No fuckin' wonder, he moaned to himself, this is unbelievable.

They started getting into it. No fancy stuff, just stroking steadily away with plenty of kissing, licking and caressing thrown in, then it started to get too good. Les pulled out, got a towel from Susie's en suite and wiped some of the sweat from them. Then he slipped a pillow under Susie's behind, lifted her legs up again and went for it; slowly at first, then his legs started going like pistons. Susie squealed and howled, Les tried not to roar as his mouth hung open and he clenched his eyes tight with the sweet pain. Then he hit the vinegar strokes, gave it one last burst, and with a howl emptied out, nearly snapping his spine as well as dislocating Susie's kneecaps. It was that good, Norton didn't know whether to laugh, cry or settle for a mild heart attack.

They flopped on the bed in a lather of sweat; Les managed to use the towel again, then dragged a sheet over them and they both lay there. Susie seemed to have crashed, Norton was almost in a state of shock; that was one of the most sensational, yet sensuous, sessions of sex Les had ever had. It was beautiful and what made it better was that Susie was an old friend. And to think, she just lived round the corner and she was coming back in a week. He winked at a shaft of light coming through the curtained window behind the bed. Thanks again, boss. I love it when you throw these little favours my way. Susie appeared to be snoring softly and happily, so Les thought he might check out her bedroom.

There wasn't a great deal to see. The old double bed was solid wood with a built-in light and, behind it, a thick black curtain was drawn across a sliding glass door that led onto the long, narrow balcony. There was a big wardrobe and a dressing table; the bed had a blue doona and faced the en suite. A few indoor plants sat in the corners and a few framed photos and smaller posters hung on the wall. The only thing unusual was a large, framed map of the universe and all the galaxies and constellations on the wall next to the bed. Like the kitchen, the bedroom was spotlessly clean and the bed was very comfortable. Les let out a contented yawn and smiled to himself. Yes, this will certainly do me for a week. Les was thinking about taking a nap when he remembered he'd promised to take Susie to the airport before long. He gave her a gentle nudge.

'Hey, Susie. How're you feeling?'

Susie snuggled her head into Norton's chest. 'Mmmmhhh! Good.'

'Don't forget you got to catch the plane at seven.'

Susie's eyes blinked open. 'Shit! What time is it?'

'It's getting on for two.'

'Two? Shit! I've still got things to pack and I have to make a heap of phone calls.'

Les drew Susie to him, gave her a tender kiss and

ran his hand over her backside. 'Do you think we could find time for . . .'

Susie pushed him away. 'No! Definitely not! In fact, you shouldn't even be here in the first place. You took advantage of me.'

'Advantage?'

'Yes, you bastard. I was weak after that walk and you mercilessly seduced me. You took advantage of a poor defenceless woman. Bastard.'

'Yeah, that's right. Blame me.' Les narrowed his eyes at Susie. 'Okay then, that's it. I've been insulted. I'm not staying here now.' Les made a half-hearted attempt to get up. Susie grabbed him.

'Come here, you big shit.' She kissed Les sweetly. 'Do you want to know the honest truth, Les?'

'Always, Susie.'

'That was one of the best things to happen to me in yonks. You got under my guard with that massage. But, boy, it was worth it.' Susie kissed Les again.

Norton kissed her in return. 'And I'm glad I bumped into you, too, Susie. In fact, I can't wait for you to get back from Melbourne. Especially now that you're rich.'

They had a bit of a cuddle and a tease. Les was rapt. Susie was pretty happy, too. It had been a good day and no better a way for two old friends to catch up again. Finally it was time to make a move. Susie wrapped the towel around her and headed for the en suite. Les climbed into his shorts and T-shirt.

'I'll go round and get my car,' he said, 'and pack up a few things I'll need while I'm here. By the time I get back you should be about ready to go. We got heaps of time.'

'To tell you the truth, Les,' replied Susie, 'I wouldn't mind leaving a bit early. Say, five. I have to meet somebody at the airport.'

'Okay.'

Les gave her a quick peck, said he'd see her when he got back and let himself out. He heard the shower running in the en suite as he walked round the front and wouldn't have minded being in there helping out with a loof. In barely five minutes Norton was at the front door of his place.

The mess was still piled up in the kitchen, in fact, if anything, there was more, and Warren and Isola were home and having a root somewhere. But where? The stereo had been left on FM and was playing in the lounge so no one heard Les come in or start tippytoeing around. He looked everywhere, but couldn't find them. Then Les snapped his fingers. The most obvious place and he'd missed it. He tip toed along the hallway and put his ear to Warren's bedroom door. Inside he could hear this very faint squealing and a low, muffled moaning and groaning. Mmmhh, thought Les after a few moments, the rooting seems to be getting very low key. I can't see our two star-crossed lovers lasting till Saturday at that rate. Oh well, who gives a stuff anyway? I'm out of here. Les listened for a moment or two more, then walked down to his room and started throwing the things he thought he'd need in a large overnight bag. He tossed in some T-shirts, socks, gym gear, stuff to wear at work, shaving tackle, etc. Not a real lot; he was only staying at Susie's for six days, not leading an expedition up Mount Everest. Les was in an extra-good mood as he packed and sort of whistled softly to himself. It was almost like going on a week's holiday, and bumping into Susie like that would put a smile on anybody's face. Before long, he felt he had everything he needed, including the latest Paul Mann novel, *The Ganja Coast*.

Les was about to leave, when he felt a rumble in his stomach and a short, sharp fart slipped out. The heavy bit of early afternoon porking had loosened him up and Les suddenly felt in need of a crap. And better to have one here than stink up poor Susie's place. He walked down to the bathroom, only to find the door locked. From the sound of the way the water was hitting the bottom of the bowl, Les tipped it to be Isola. He waited a moment, then absently walked back into the kitchen.

Les peered around at the mess, the flies and the large box of Kleenex tissues sitting next to the kitchen phone, then farted again. The second one was a lot louder, hotter and smellier than the first one. Norton stared at the box of tissues, shrugged his shoulders and thought, well, why bloody not? After all, it is my house. I own it, and being the said owner I can do what I like. Can't I? Yes, Les, of course you can. Les took off his shorts and Speedos, climbed up and straddled his arse across the kitchen sink and shat all over the dirty dishes. About three good-sized turds. Shit! I needed that crap more than I thought, mused Les as he climbed back down. He wiped his date with the Kleenex tissues and dropped them on the pile of fresh, steaming turds. I'll bet they don't even notice it, thought Les as he put his shorts back on. Then he squinted his eyes. Christ! They'd have to. If Norton's two farts were bad, the crap was diabolical. It took the

31

flies around the kitchen tidy about two seconds to zero in on it for the picnic of their lives. Les didn't bother to wash his hands in the sink. But he did open the back door in case there were any other flies outside who might like to join their friends in the kitchen for a free smorgasbord. Feeling better, and lighter, Les tip toed into his room, got his bag and crept quietly out the front door. The bathroom was still occupied as he left.

There was a parking spot just out the front of Susie's, so Les didn't bother to use the garage. He eased his old Ford ute in behind a white four-wheel drive, entered the security door outside, knocked on Susie's, waited a few moments, then decided to let himself in.

Susie was sitting on a footstool near the TV in the corner, talking to someone on the phone. She'd changed into black corduroy jeans, boots and a thick, red-check hangout shirt. In the lounge, a tan leather jacket was thrown over a suitcase; it might have been summer, but Susie *was* going to Melbourne. She gave Les a quick wave. Les winked back, put his bag down next to an overnight bag that looked like it was full of CDs, and sat on the lounge. There was what sounded like a nice CD playing softly. Kind of Santana without the screaming guitar, and no vocals. Pleasant, cruisy music. Les settled back, listened to the music and half-earwigged Susie on the phone. It sounded like a woman called Carol. Finally Susie hung up.

'Oh, boy. That was my sister. Can she talk! I see you brought your stuff.'

Les nodded.

Susie smiled. 'One more phone call.'

Les watched her dial and settled into the music playing. It was still very laid-back, but good. From snatches, he could hear Susie was talking to some bloke called Joe. Les felt like going over and rattling through the CDs to see just what was there, but felt it might not be too prudent with the landlady in the room. Finally Susie got off the blower.

'I gotta meet that bloke at the airport.' She looked at Les. 'So how's things?'

'Good,' said Les. 'I'm stoked having somewhere nice to stay while all that rattle's going on round my place. Plus it's good I can do an old china plate a favour at the same time.'

'Does Warren know you're staying here?'

Les nodded happily. 'Yeah, I left him a message in the kitchen.'

'Good.' Susie got up, sat on the lounge next to Les and gave him a bit of a cuddle. Norton had to smile. 'Now, no bringing any low molls back here. And no parties.'

'I was thinking of ringing this Albanian I know in the Cross and shooting a couple of porn videos while you're away. Is that okay?'

'Just as long as there's something in the whack for me.' Susie gave Les a bit of a clip over the ear. 'No. I trust you.' She looked at her watch. 'We got a bit of time. You feel like a coffee or something?'

'Not so much a coffee,' answered Les.

'Okay then. How about a nice cup of lime tea?'

'Sounds . . .'

Les was about to finish when Susie pushed him to his feet. 'Hey, Les,' she said, moving him over to the sliding glass door. 'That's those two Russian blokes I was telling you about.' Les got a quick glimpse of two men walking slowly along the footpath. 'Quick, into the kitchen.'

Les followed Susie into the kitchen and they looked through the thin curtain, half drawn back on the kitchen window. In a moment, two men in grey track-suits, carrying fishing rods, came crunching up the pathway. One was taller and older than the other, very jowly and thick-chested — a bit like Boris Yeltsin but with scrubbier, slightly darker hair. Les tipped him to be around fifty. The other man was younger, around thirty, same dark hair with a lean, brooding face that seemed to match a lean, fit-looking body. He appeared to move and walk with a brisk, almost military style. The older man fumbled for the key to the front door, said something in Russian to the younger man, then they let themselves in and tromped up the stairs.

Susie turned away from the window. 'That's them,' she almost whispered.

'So what?' shrugged Norton. 'They just look like two blokes gone fishing to me. What's the big deal?'

'Wait till you see old Maca out the front. He'll tell you about them.'

'Old Maca?'

'Yeah. Macabee. He's an old Russian Jew sits out the front. Likes to keep an eye on things. He spits and curses at them. When they've gone past, of course. He told me they were nogoodniks.'

'All right,' conceded Les, 'I'll keep an eye on them. If they get out of line, I'll shoot the both of them. If they've got any fish, I'll put them in the deep freeze.'

'Do that, Les. And put your big boofhead in there as well. We'd hate to have what's left of your brain over-heat.' Susie smiled up at Les and rubbed her hands together. 'Now, how about that cup of lime tea?'

'Sounds good to me.' Les sat in the kitchen and watched as Susie got the kettle and things together, while the same CD played in the lounge.

'Hey, that's not a bad CD playing, Susie,' he said. 'Who's that?'

'The Rippingtons. "Kilimanjaro". It's not bad is it?'

'Yeah. It's kind of boppy cool. I like it.'

'There's another three there besides that.'

'I'll tape them for sure.'

The lime tea sitting in his cup looked exactly like piss and didn't taste much better; kind of bitter-sweet and almost undrinkable, even with a dollop of honey. Les wished he'd had coffee, although Susie seemed to be enjoying hers. They nattered on for a while about this and that. Susie said there was a number next to the phone where Les could get in touch if he wanted to and she'd ring now and again herself.

Before long it was time to go. Les took Susie's bags and carried them out to the car. To avoid confusion and any trauma, Les decided to let Susie punch in the numbers on the security system.

The traffic was a little heavier than Les had expected and it was getting on for 5.30 when they pulled up at the domestic terminal. Susie seemed a little anxious and was in a hurry to get out of the car, considering her flight didn't leave till seven.

'Do you need any help?' asked Les. 'I can go and get you a trolley.'

'No, it's all right.' Susie grabbed her suitcase and handbag and slung the bag of CDs over her shoulder.

Les adjusted the strap a little and gave her a quick but affectionate kiss. 'I'll see you when you get back.'

'Sunday night, Les.' Susie gave Les a quick peck in return. 'You know where that number is if you need me in Melbourne.'

Les grinned. 'No worries,' he nodded.

Susie turned and hurried for the door. As Les got back in his car he noticed a dark-haired man in jeans approach Susie as she walked inside. He said something to her briefly, then took her overnight bag and was gone. Les nodded once more. Yeah, I didn't really think you'd need me to help you with your luggage, Side Valve, old pal.

Norton drove to Bondi Junction, got a park in Bronte Road, then walked down to one of those Low-Cost places and got a dozen ninety-minute cassettes. He was about to have a freshly squeezed orange juice when he bumped into a couple of blokes he used to play football with that he hadn't seen for a while. They'd just won some money at the TAB and were going over to Billy The Pigs for a steak and a few beers. If Les wanted to join them, they'd shout. Not being a man to knock back a free feed and happy to catch up with a couple of old mates, Les did just that. Consequently it wasn't getting any earlier when Les got back to Susie's and all the parking spaces were gone out the front. Les cruised down the driveway, hit the buzzer and the security door creaked and rumbled open in its own sweet time. Susie's garage wasn't the biggest in the world but with a bit of twisting and turning, Les was able to get the old ute into it and a minute later he was inside the unit.

He stacked the dozen bottles of Toohey's long necks he'd bought when he left The Pigs into the fridge, then unpacked his clothes and hung them in Susie's wardrobe alongside her dresses and jackets. I wonder if there's anything in there might fit me, he mused. Les shook his head. No, I doubt it. And I don't like her colour sense all that much anyway. Some of her handbags aren't bad though. He grabbed his towel and shaving gear and headed for the shower.

Susie's bathroom was about half as big as Les's with a frosted, glass shower cabinet, separate bath and a toilet. Like the kitchen, it was spotlessly clean with a few indoor plants and little, fluffy women's do-dads here and there, plus jars of cotton buds and dried flowers and things around the bathroom sink and mirror. Les had a shave, then changed into a pair of jocks and a plain white T-shirt. He got a beer from the fridge and stood in front of all the CDs. He was tempted to get into the music straight away, but he had all week and there was a programme about old American gangsters he wanted to watch on SBS, plus they were having a repeat double-header of *KYTV*. Norton switched the TV on and settled back.

By the time they'd finished Les had knocked off four beers and he was starting to yawn and there was no way he was going to watch the late movie on SBS — *The Revenge of Grudnar the Crab Sheller* — a tormented drama of conflict and intrigue in a seventeenth-century Icelandic fish factory. Les switched off the TV and went into the bedroom. He switched on the lamp behind Susie's bed and pulled the curtains shut tight.

He cleaned his teeth and let go a couple more yawns, then climbed into Susie's bed, switched off the light and closed his eyes. The bed was comfortable, so were the pillows, and Les felt pretty good. So what's on tomorrow? he thought as he began to drift off. Nothing really. Train in the morning, tape music most of the day and work that night — if you could call it that. Les was lying there happily when something made him open his eyes. Susie's big poster of the universe was luminous and you could see all the constellations and galaxies quite clearly against the wall in the darkened room. It was almost like standing out in the countryside on a crystal clear night and it was quite fascinating. Les stared at it for a while and before long he was drifting along somewhere in the cosmos himself.

It was after eight the next morning by the time Les surfaced, got cleaned up and wandered into Susie's kitchen wearing his faded Levi shorts and a white T-shirt. He had woken up earlier and was lying in bed half asleep thinking how sweet it all was, when some bloke arrived in an old mini-van and started whipper-snippering the front lawn. And with Susie's unit being right at the front, the machine sounded like it was about a metre from Norton's head. There were plenty of goodies, sauces and pickles in the landlady's fridge. Les settled on some Roman focaccia, which he toasted with cottage cheese, sliced tomato and onion and a splash of salsa, and washed down with a plunger of New Guinea Blue. Peering out the kitchen window while the kettle boiled, he noticed it didn't look like too bad a day outside. A bit of a southerly blowing again with some clouds around; pretty much like the day before. Les took his breakfast over to the kitchen table and got stuck into it, and couldn't help but think again how sweet it all was.

Susie had a small radio on the table tuned to AM.

Les switched it on and while he was eating, all he seemed to get was these three miserable radio announcers ripping into greenies. It was one non-stop tirade interrupted only by commercials and Les couldn't believe so much venom could pour out of one tiny speaker. All some poor souls were trying to do was stop what's left of the rainforests from being turned into chopsticks and glossy wrapping for the Japanese so a couple of hundred beer-bellied truck drivers could keep their jobs. But the way these radio wallies had whipped themselves into a lather, you'd have thought the greenies were ruining the economy, raping women in the streets and throwing babies up in the air and catching them on bayonets while they ran around growing pot everywhere. When the announcers weren't howling for the communist, tree-hugging greenie scums' blood, they were mentally stalking the Minister for the Environment and wanting to hang him up by his heels with piano wire over a slow fire too. He was some kind of crazed, woozy heterodox just for holding his portfolio in the first place and having the unmitigated gall to argue against their carping, didactic bullshit. Norton gave the tirade about another minute, then shook his head and switched the radio off.

Communist, greenie, tree-hugging bastards. Les took a sip of coffee and turned around in his chair. Haven't me and Warren got a photo in the kitchen of Dick Smith with his arms around a tree? Bloody oath we have. Next to that one of the two dolphins jumping in front of the ship. And what's that goose call greenies? Watermelons? Green on the outside and red in the middle. I know what would be a good nickname for him and his prima donna mates. Chinese Gardens. All sweet-smelling and nicely manicured on top, but full of shit underneath. Norton turned back to the now-silent talkback radio. No. What a man should do is write a letter to the paper about those clowns. But what could you say? And in a way you do have to feel sorry for them, I suppose. Take that first bloke. He'd be dirty on environmentalists because there's no way he could ever pronounce the word properly. And the other bloke. Well, let's be honest. If you were born with a face like that you'd be filthy on mother nature too. And the last bloke? Shit! That's a hard one. I know. Greenies get arrested near leafy trees. He got pinched near a lavatory. Les, you're a dead-set genius. Norton raised his cup of coffee that was now starting to get cold. Trouble is, when it comes to writing letters, I'm flat out writing the date. And talking about the date — Les snatched a quick glance at his watch — I've got things to do, places to go and tapes to tape. And it ain't getting no earlier.

Les finished the last of his breakfast, then cleaned up as scrupulously as possible, hoping it would pass the landlady's muster when she came back from Melbourne. One thing, mused Les as he wiped the sink for the third time, no matter how I leave the kitchen, it couldn't look any worse than mine was when I left it.

When he finished washing and wiping, Les thought he might give Billy Dunne a ring and tell him what was going on. He wouldn't see his loyal workmate till Thursday night when they worked together and Billy might get a laugh from his fellow workmate's situation. Les walked into the lounge, sat down on the same footstool as Susie had and pushed the buttons on the phone.

'Hello,' came a familiar voice at the other end.

'Hello, Billy. It's Les. How are you, mate?'

'Les? Shit! Where have you been? I've been trying to ring you.'

'You have?'

'Yeah, so's Price. And what's up with Warren? Has he got asthma or something?'

Norton's shoulders gave a bit of a ripple. 'No. He's . . .'

'Anyway, don't worry about it. Are you at home now?'

'No, I'm at Side Valve Susie's joint. I'm looking after it for her while she's away.'

There was silence on the end of the line for a moment. 'Side Valve Susie? That hairdresser from Melbourne?'

'Yeah. I'm staying here till Sunday while she's down there seeing her family.'

'Aaah! That's where you've been.'

'So what's all the drama anyway?' enquired Les. 'You've been ringing me. And El Presidente himself.'

'Yeah. And Eddie. And George.'

'Fuck! What's . . .?'

'You'll find out at work tonight. I'll be there and we're getting them all out by eleven. Earlier if possible.'

'Shit! We're talking emergency procedures here, Billy. What's going on, mate?'

There was a silence on the end of the line for a moment. 'Hello? This is a phone you're using, isn't it? What was your name again? Clarry, is it? I think you've got the wrong number, Mr Clarry. Hello?'

Les nodded. 'I think I get the picture. Okay, Gunther. I'll see you at the pickle factory.'

'Auf Wiedersehen. Unt ebrytink gut for you and de family too plis.'

'Yeah. Danke.'

Les hung up and stared at the phone. Well, I wonder what the bloody hell that's all about. Christ! It's been as quiet as buggery at the club lately. Nothing even like a drama, and we're not really doing anything illegal anyway. No money changes hands. It's all done on credit. As long as your credit's okay, nothing illegal happens to you.

Les stood up, drew back the curtain and looked at the trees running down Hall Street towards Six Ways. Ahh! It's probably nothing. And Price does like to bung on the odd drama now and again. Though I hope Eddie doesn't have to go out and kill some bloke. That can be a pain in the arse at times. Norton shrugged. Oh, well, whatever it is, I'll know tonight. In the meantime, I have to at least make an effort. Les put his training gear in his bag, secured the flat and headed out the front door for North Bondi Surf Club.

Seated on the corner of the brick fence out front was a dumpy little bloke with a pot belly and a florid, grumpy face half-hidden behind a pair of wide-framed glasses. He was wearing an untidy grey and orange tracksuit and shafts of silver hair spread from beneath a blue Roosters cap. He was looking around, checking the people out carefully without quite taking down passing numberplates. Les tipped him to be old Macabee.

'Hello, boss' said Les as he walked past.

The old Russian was looking over Hall Street and stared up. 'Boss? What is boss?' he said in a guttural growl. 'I not boss.'

'Sorry, mate. No offence. But you just remind me of a boss I had once when I worked in a pork factory.'

'No boss,' said Macabee without expression. 'Just livink here.'

'Uh huh!' nodded Les. 'Well, I'm looking after Miss Susie's flat for her while she's away.'

'Yes, she tell me this.'

'My name's Les anyway.' Norton offered his hand.

The old Russian held up his hand and it felt like squeezing half a kilogram of warm suet. 'I am Macabee.'

'Pleased to meet you, Macabee.'

Les was about to say goodbye or something before he got on his way when the front door opened and the two Russians Susie had pointed out came walking along the pathway towards them, wearing the same grey tracksuits, and carrying the same fishing rods and bags over their shoulders.

Les made eye contact with the older, bigger one. 'Morning,' he said and smiled.

'Good morning, my friend,' beamed the Russian. 'Is good day, yes?'

'Yeah. Not bad.' Les gave the other Russian a nod and got a curt, thin smile in reply. Both men ignored Macabee and Macabee seemed to be enjoying doing the same. 'So off for a bit of fishin', are you?' asked Les.

'Yes. Fishing is good, but —' the big Russian started

to laugh, '— most times ve are finishink up mit vot you Aussies say — the vet arse and no fishes.'

Norton laughed. 'Yeah, that's about it, mate. A wet khyber and no Lillian Gish.'

The big Russian caught the eye of the other one. 'Goodbye, my friend,' he said, and walked off roaring with wheezy laughter at his own joke.

'They don't seem like a couple of bad blokes,' Les said to Macabee, curious as to what his reaction would be.

Macabee snorted, then spat on the ground. 'Caechibi bastards!'

'Well, I don't know where they come from. Mongolia, Chechnya, Chaebi or wherever. They're all Russians to me, boss.'

Macabee gave an impassive nod of his head.

'Anyway. I have to get going. I'll see you, mate.'

'Mmmhhh.'

Well, isn't he just a happy, tap-dancing little Vegemite, thought Les, as he strolled down Hall Street. You don't have to be Einstein to see what's going on. Wogs with their dopey bloody ethnic rivalries. He's crooked on those two because they're Chibi bastards or whatever. And they hate the Russians who hate the Chechnyans. It just goes on and on until they run out of people to kill. Norton shook his head. Why don't you try and be like that young Russian fighter, Macabee, you silly old goat, and leave it all back there.

After stopping for the paper and a freshly squeezed orange juice, Les was at North Bondi Surf Club, changed and ready for two hours of torture. Norton did pretty much the same as the day before. Only, instead of the swim, he went for a paddle with 'The T-shirt' to Wedding Cake Island and back. The T-shirt was a full-on clubbie and extra good in the paddling rort so the conversation was pretty limited as they stroked along, with Norton doing his best to keep up. Fortunately the southerly was with them on the return journey so Norton was able to get a bit of a mag going.

However, when they got back to the surf club, Les put the heavy bag on hold and settled for a few stretches and chin-ups and that in the exercise station next door.

Feeling in a pretty good mood after he'd showered, and seeing The T-shirt was such good company on the paddle, Les offered to buy him lunch over at Speedo's. The Shirt didn't have to start work till three and, being a bit like Norton, wasn't one to knock back a free lunch either. So over to Speedo's they went, where they knocked over salads, omelettes, more focaccia and plenty of Speedo's A1 coffee. Before long they were both bloated and it was time to get going. The Shirt thanked Les for the scoff; Norton said he'd prob-ably see him down the surf club for some more pun-ishment tomorrow.

By the time Les got back to Susie's unit and soaked his sweaty gym gear in the laundry, the day was start-ing to slip away. He poured a glass of mineral water and glanced through the *Telegraph Mirror* only to find Piers Akerman putting the boot into greenies too. Christ! What is this? thought Les. Open season? The way things are going, the greenies'll finish up an endangered species just like the poor bloody things they're trying to protect. And wouldn't the Japs and the

46

developers love that. Oh well. At least Akerman isn't as biased and bad-mouthed as those other creeps. Les closed the paper, finished his drink of water and went into the lounge room.

Now, where do I bloody start? he wondered, tearing the wrapping off a cassette as he stared at all the CDs; there were hundreds to choose from. Oh well. Just pick some out, run them through and see what I come up with. Susie's CD was a five-stack and you could tape and switch tracks off the remote. Before long, Les had the stacker filled and was spinning the CDs around, taping the tracks he liked best and writing the names down in a notebook.

With a bit of mucking around and a couple more glasses of mineral water, Les was able to get three ninety-minute tapes filled by late afternoon. It would have been nice just to sit back and listen to all the different music, but Les did some more stretches and a bit of yoga for his back while he was taping. Some of Susie's CDs were a bit iffy, but most of them were great. There were bands and singers he'd never heard of before; and if he had there were CDs and tracks they had out that he'd never heard. Billy Burnette, Lonnie Mack, Mark Collie, Bob Margolin. Ron Levy's 'Wild Kingdom', The Smokin' Joe Kubek Band, Asleep At The Wheel, Nathan and the Zydeco Cha Chas. All good boogieing stuff. A track by Lou Reed, 'The Original Wrapper', surprised him, as did one by Ian Hunter, 'Big Time'. But one track did get Les. 'Baby Likes to Boogie Like a Boggie Woogie Choo-Choo Train' by The Tractors. He played it three times in a row before taping it, then played it again. Les even put

47

down 'Rescue Me' by Fontalla Bass because it reminded him of the time he met DD on the Gold Coast and they hustled to it. And a track by Sunrize Band from the NT, 'Bugula Gun Bachira'. The whole album was good and the best thing was you couldn't understand a word they were saying. All up, not a bad way to put in an afternoon, and Les had barely scratched the surface of the CDs yet.

Outside, it wasn't much of a day now, with light rain on and off. People and families walked past out the front. Macabee seemed to vanish, then come back again. The two Russian fishermen returned; Les paid them scant attention but they didn't appear to be loaded down with too many fish. Les made a cup of tea and a bit of toast; he wasn't all that hungry and if he did get peckish later on, there were always plenty of sandwiches and things at the club. Before long, it was time for a shave and the big Queenslander was standing in front of the TV wearing a pair of jeans, blue T-shirt, matching windcheater and a pair of black grunge boots watching the last of the news on the ABC.

There had been no phone calls and no sign of Susie's boarder. Talking about boarders. Norton smiled down at the phone and wondered if he could still disguise his voice. He picked up the receiver, pushed the buttons and waited.

'Hello,' came a dull woman's voice at the other end, which had to be Isola.

'Could I spik plis to Mr Norton?' No matter how hard Les tried, it always sounded like a Jewish Humphrey Bogart.

'He is not here.'

'Den ver is he?'

'I don't know.'

'Vot you mean, you don't know?'

'I don't know because I do not. I am just here staying.'

'Den vy don't you find out ver he is, you dopey moll, so I can be leaving him a message.'

There was a pause for a moment. 'Vot you just said?'

'I said I vont to leave Mr Norton a message. Don't you got no brains, you vombat?'

'Vot? I got der brains.'

'Yeah. I am vishing you had a brain as big as your cunt, you dill. I vas told an elephant could valk into your cunt vit a mahmout on top carrying an umbrella.'

'Vot! You don't talk to me like that. Who are you?'

'You don't like the vay I talk to you?'

'No. I don't like.'

'Well, if you don't like,' Norton roared into the phone, 'why don't you fuck off!' Then he hung up.

Les looked down at the receiver and smiled. He was hoping to get Warren, but that would have to do for the time being. Well look at that — Norton's eyes went from the phone to his watch — it's about time I went and bundied on at the pickle factory. Norton locked the unit up as securely as possible and, knowing there would more than likely be a drink on if they had a meeting after the club closed, strolled down to Six Ways and caught a taxi.

It was drizzling rain when Les got out of the cab, knocked their special knock on the club door and let himself in with his key. Billy was dressed pretty much like Norton and sitting on a stool reading a book called *Real Cops* by Brett Stevens. He smiled up and closed his book as Les let shut the door behind him.

'Les, how are you, mate?'

'All right, Billy. How's y'self?'

'Good. You look like you've been doing a bit of training.'

'Yeah. That fuckin' T-shirt took me for a paddle on a ski. He near killed me. What did you do today?'

'Did a bit of work on the house. Took the kids to soccer. I ended up doing about an hour in my gym.' Billy gave Les a bit of grin, followed by a left rip that pulled up just near Norton's ribs. 'So what's all this with Side Valve Susie? I told Price where you rang me from.'

'Yeah, I'm looking after her place for her till Sunday. Up in little Leningrad with all these crazy Russians.'

Les filled Billy in on what was going on. About the session with Susie, the old bloke out the front of the flats. What was going on at Chez Norton's and how he left the place when he packed his gear.

'So, that's about it, William. I'm in this flat taping all these grouse CDs and having a nice rest. It's rather delightful actually.'

Billy stared at Les and shook his head. 'You're unbelievable.'

'Yeah,' a quick smile flicked across Norton's lips, 'I do have my moments, I suppose. But what's all the drama about? That's more important than me bumping into an old flame and having a dump in my kitchen sink.'

Billy made a gesture with his hands. 'I don't know myself, to tell you the truth. But there's some sort of trouble going on.'

'Somebody out to get Price? Eddie got to do a job?'

Billy shook his head. 'No, I don't think it's anything like that, but it does sound important.'

Les thought for a moment. 'Oh, well, I imagine we'll know tonight. Anyway, I'd better go up and let them know I'm here. They all up there?'

'Yeah,' nodded Billy.

'Okay. I'll see you after.' Les jogged off up the stairs.

There was hardly anyone in the club; a dozen or so well-dressed punters seated at two tables playing Manilla. The two girls in their black uniforms, with the sandwiches and drinks, were standing near one of the windows; they gave Les a dainty wave when they saw him come up the stairs. At one of the tables Les saw Price, half with his back to him, in a neat grey suit and maroon tie. He wasn't playing cards, just watching. George Brennan was at the other table in a dark suit and matching tie doing much the same thing. He saw Les and winked; Les winked back, then walked softly over to Price. It was quiet in the club. Some of the men playing cards saw Les and looked up for a brief instant then returned to their game. Les moved up behind Price and tapped him gently on one shoulder.

Price looked up and smiled. 'Hello, mate,' he said quietly. 'How's it going?'

'All right.' Les winked back.

Having let Price know he was there, Norton walked over to the two sandwich girls, had a quick word and a

51

bit of a joke, then started walking unobtrusively round the club. He checked the windows, the doors, the toilets, the fire escape. Gave the punters the once-over, then walked around all the windows again. If anybody wanted to know what he was doing, Norton was doing exactly what was required of him. His job. Noticing a movement through one of the frosted glass windows in the office, Les walked over, knocked gently on the door, then opened it. Eddie was sitting there on the phone, dressed pretty much like Les, only he was wearing a black leather jacket. Les gave him a wave, got a quick wave in return, then closed the office door again. Norton had one more look round the place, then, satisfied everything appeared to be in order, walked back down the stairs to Billy.

'Well. Everything seems okay up there.'

'Mmmhh.' Billy looked up from his book. 'I had a look around earlier.'

'S'pose we may as well just hang down here. Then go up and put our heads in every now and again.'

Billy nodded in agreement. 'You got something to read?'

'Yeah, I have, as a matter of fact,' replied Les, pulling his copy of *The Ganja Coast* from his jacket pocket.

'Good. Tell me when it's my turn to go upstairs.'

Billy went back to his tales of cops and situations in Australia. Les opened up his book of hippies and drugs in India.

About five minutes or so went by, then Billy spoke.

'What's that book like? Any good?'

'Yeah, it's not bad,' replied Les. 'How's yours?'

'All right, yeah.'

They didn't let any more people in the club. Anybody that showed up was politely turned away. There was a dangerous electrical fault; but everything would be in order by tomorrow night. Sorry about the inconvenience, you should always ring, just in case. Good night, have a safe trip home in the rain and we might see you tomorrow. The rest of the punters were out by eleven, along with the sandwich girls; the lights were dimmed, the club was secured and they were all in the office — Price behind his desk, Les on his right, Billy on his left, George was spread across the lounge and Eddie was on a seat not quite next to him. All the 'hellos' and 'how are yous' were dispensed with, everyone was comfortable with a drink in their hand and now it was down to business.

'All right, oh grand vizier,' said Les to Price. 'So what have you got your bowels in an uproar over this time? Have I got to go and bash some poor kids cause they've been skateboarding on your driveway? What's up, mate?'

Price held up his hand. 'Hey! Before we go any further. What's your domestic circumstances at the moment? Are you staying at some sheila's place or something? Billy gave me half the story.'

'That's right,' nodded Les. 'An old friend of mine — Susie. I'm looking after her flat for her while she's away. Till Sunday.'

'On your own?' asked Price.

'Yeah. On my Pat Malone. There's a boarder, but he's away somewhere.'

53

Price glanced over at Eddie. 'That could come in very handy.'

Eddie nodded back almost imperceptibly.

Les took a sip from his bottle of Eumundi Lager and looked at his watch. 'So, come on, what's all the drama? I should be home in bed now watching David Letterman.'

'Yeah. Playing with your dick'd be more like it,' said George Brennan over his Bacardi and grapefruit juice.

'True,' Les nodded again, 'but at the moment I got someone doesn't mind doing it for me. So I don't have to bother.'

Price eased back in his chair, which somehow only seemed to emphasise his presence in the room more. He took a sip from his Scotch and soda. 'Okay, Les. So you want to know what's going on?'

'Yeah,' answered Les, 'I wouldn't mind. Especially if it concerns my health and wellbeing. Not to mention my job security here at the Sydney Harbour bridge club.'

'Fair enough.' Price paused for a moment, looking evenly at Norton. 'So where have you been hanging out lately, Les? Down on Bondi Beach, I suppose?'

'Yeah,' replied Norton again. 'I go down the beach.'

'Whereabouts? Down the south end?'

'Yeah, though the north end mainly. But I go down the south end sometimes.'

'And what do you see when you're down the south end, Les?'

Norton shrugged. 'I dunno. Wogs kickin' soccer balls. Westie yobbos kickin' footballs. Poofs throwin' tennis balls around. Tits, bums. Blokes with the cut lunches stuffed into G-strings. The usual.'

'Yeah, but what else is down there?' continued Price.

Les shrugged again. 'Waxheads, Japs riding lids and takin' photos. Blokes sellin' ice-creams. Hey, what the fuck is this?' said Les, looking around the room. 'The Spanish Inquisition, because I hang down the south end now and again. What's going on?'

'Settle down, Les,' soothed Price, continuing to stare at Norton. 'But what else do you see when you're down there?'

'Just up to the right a bit,' cut in George.

'Just up to the right?' Les shrugged again. 'The stormwater drain. The baths?'

There was a quick round of applause. 'The man is hot,' said Eddie, raising his Stolichnaya and lemon. 'Go, Les. Smokin'.'

'That's right, Les,' said Price. 'The Bondi baths. Now, Les. What else have you noticed sitting on the Bondi baths? Take your time, mate. The buzzer doesn't go for another ten seconds.'

'Oh, I don't bloody know,' said Norton, shaking his head. 'The bloody Icebergs?'

There was another round of applause. 'I told you the kid was a genius,' said Price, smiling around at the others. 'Now, Les. If you've read the papers and that, and just looked around, what have you noticed about the Bondi baths and the Bondi Icebergs?'

'The 'Bergs? They're kicking them out and pulling the whole place down. The bulldozers go in next week or something.' Les looked around the room. 'But what the fuck's this got to do with me? I'm not a member. I've only been in the place a few times for a drink or maybe a game of handball, and I have a swim in the baths about twice a year if I'm lucky. To be honest. I don't give a stuff what they do with the place. It looked pretty fucked the last time I was in there.'

'Have you ever walked round the back of the baths, Les?' asked Eddie, carefully sipping his vodka.

'Yeah,' grunted Norton, not so carefully sipping his beer.

'And what did you discover when you were around there, grasshopper?' asked George.

Les turned to George. 'Fucked if I know, oh fat priest from the temple. Dog shit everywhere, a care-taker's flat. A bloody old handball court . . .'

'Yeah, baby!' Price led the applause this time, which was a little more sustained. When the clapping died down, it seemed quieter than ever in the office and Price was still staring at Norton. 'And do you know what's under that handball court, Les?' he asked quietly.

Norton shook his head. He didn't know. He didn't want to know. He didn't want an answer, but he knew he was going to get one. 'No. What?' he replied dully.

'Two bodies.'

'Two bodies?' repeated Les.

'That's right,' nodded Price. 'And we're going to get them out this Friday night.'

Les closed his eyes for a second, then stared back at Price. 'Let me get this straight. There's two bodies underneath the handball court at the Icebergs and you want to get them out this Friday night?'

56

'That's right,' said Price.

'How?' asked Norton, knowing he needn't have bothered asking.

'Explosives,' said Eddie.

Norton slumped back in his seat trying his level best not to let his presence be felt. 'You're fuckin' kidding.'

'No, we're not,' said Eddie. 'Not in the least.'

George Brennan shook his head at Les. 'Not unless you want to be visiting Uncle Price and the rest of us on weekends for about the next twenty years.'

'That's right, Les,' agreed Price. 'And we need you to give us a hand.'

Billy Dunne nodded slowly. 'We're all in this one, mate. All hands on deck.'

Norton closed his eyes again and slumped further back into his seat. 'Oh shit!'

'Hey. Don't sweat it, hero,' said George. 'Eddie's got a sensational genius plan.'

'Eddie's got a plan.' Les drained his beer, got up, dumped the empty in the bin and made himself a nice, strong George Dickle and Diet Coke, then sat back down again. 'So what's the plan, Eddie?'

Eddie took another sip of vodka. 'We're gonna do it at ten o'clock this Friday night. I got a bloke lined up. He's the best in the business.'

'Hey, hang on a second,' cut in Les, 'just out of curiosity, who are the two bodies? I mean, if I'm taking the odds to get tossed in the nick if this fucks up, I think I'm entitled to know.' Les turned to Price. 'Or am I just the hillbilly from Queensland. And don't tell him anything.'

'No. You're right,' conceded Price over another

Scotch and soda. 'If you're good enough to be in the dirty work, you're good enough to know the dirty details.'

'Thank you,' said Norton.

'Like I said,' continued Price. 'There're two bodies. One's a boxer — or ex-boxer would be a better description. The other's an ex-police inspector who was next in line to be Commissioner of Police.' Price took a good sip of Scotch. 'I'm not worried about the boxer so much. But if this other walloper shows up, it could turn out a bit nasty.'

'Yeah,' agreed Billy. 'Especially with all this forensic science and DNA strands and shit they got going now.'

'Exactly, Billy,' nodded Price.

Les took a glance at his watch. 'Well, come on, tell us the story. You've got me in now. And I ain't goin' nowhere and there's no shortage of piss.' Les finished his bourbon, got up for another one making the others a drink while he was there, then sat back down again.

'All right,' said Price. 'It was around Christmas 1967.' He turned to his hitman. 'You remember, Eddie.'

'Yeah, I remember,' said Eddie. 'Just before New Year's Eve.' He looked at Price. Half shook his head and half smiled. 'Yeah, I remember all right. You and your bloody . . .' Eddie was about to say something to Price but changed his mind and sort of quietly chuckled into his vodka. Price sort of smiled innocently over at Eddie then went on to relate what had happened back in the swinging sixties.

As Price had said, it was around Christmas 1967. A

boxer called Bo Bo Brooks punched Price's sister in an inner-city nightclub she was managing, because she politely told him to settle down a bit when he started playing up. Brooks was full of drink and all the goodies and didn't just punch her. He hit with a combination, breaking her jaw, her nose, and putting a dozen or so stitches in her mouth; she wasn't a very big woman and it was lucky he didn't kill her. It all happened very quickly and the hero Bo Bo ran out of the nightclub and into the night before the bouncers could get their hands on him and see how he liked boxing with a couple of broken arms and legs; and quite probably more. However, Bo Bo didn't run far. Price and Eddie caught up with him the following night holed up in Paddington, when it was more of a slummy suburb. After hitting him over the head with an iron bar Price held him while Eddie garrotted him. Then they rolled him up in an old oilskin and took him round to Price's place, before taking him away somewhere for a not-quite-decent Christian burial. No one lamented Bo Bo's disappearance and, as far as anyone knew, he skipped the country and went to America where he continued fighting under another name.

At almost the same time, two very heavy detectives in the gaming squad shot and killed a police inspector who was next in line to be head of police in NSW. The word got out he had some terminal illness and didn't have all that long to live anyway and when he made the top spot he was apparently going to turn Queen's evidence and give everybody up, including Price as well as any police or politicians involved. And then write a book before he went. This was going to be his legacy.

The two cops involved weren't complete dropkicks, just ruthless when it came to saving their own necks, plus their fellow officers' — which was the way of things back in NSW during the swinging sixties and seventies. Price owed the two detectives involved a couple of favours and was on a sort of friendly basis with them; they smothered plenty of things for him and were never too greedy. They knew Price wasn't all that keen on the late police inspector and jokingly rang him to ask if he knew a good place to get rid of the body? Price said to bring the body round to his place and he'd get rid of it for them. Not telling them he was getting rid of one himself, thus letting the two detectives think they now owed Price a big favour. They brought the body over, wrapped in an old oilskin, left some of the late inspector's fishing gear on the rocks at Malabar where he used to like fishing, and the headlines read that he disappeared while fishing, was presumed drowned and eaten by sharks. So it turned out a very nice vibe all round.

At that time Price was very fit and used to play a lot of handball; mainly at Clovelly Surf Club, but also at the Bondi Icebergs. Being a kind and generous person and knowing at the time the Icebergs were scratching a bit for money, Price had offered to build the club a new handball court. It was all excavated and laid out with several tonnes of fill stacked to one side, ready to go in before the concrete pour the following morning. The fill was stacked in such a way that if you removed the wooden poles and gave it one good heave the lot would fall in without having to use a bulldozer. Price said this would be an ideal spot to hide the bodies for two reasons. Firstly, they'd never find them under all the rubble and concrete. And secondly, Price, having a great sense of humour, reasoned that it would be nice to be able to play a few sets of handball over the top of two dropkicks he hated. Afterwards, all the people Price used to play handball with never ceased to be amazed that either win, lose or draw, Price would always dance a little soft-shoe shuffle after the game on the ocean side of the handball court.

'So that's the story, Les,' said Price, taking a sip from another Scotch and soda, then turning to Eddie. 'It was a funny old night all right.'

'Yeah, real funny,' said Eddie. 'We almost got sprung.'

'Did we what,' chimed in George.

'Sprung?' enquired Les.

'Yeah.' Eddie was a little serious. 'We dragged the two bodies down to the handball court, while George waited in this old panel van we had. And we get sprung by these two wog skindivers in wetsuits.'

'Fair dinkum?' laughed Les.

'Fair dinkum,' repeated Eddie. 'Actually I think they were in front of us. You got to remember, Les, it was pitch black and they just seemed to appear out of nowhere. They were probably out ripping off abalone and lobsters. They were carrying all their stuff with them in this big black bag and as soon as they saw us they dropped what they were carrying and pissed off. Naturally we weren't bloody hanging around. We dumped the two bodies in the hole, hit the poles holding up the fill with a sledgehammer and we're out of there in about two seconds flat before the dust even started to settle.' Eddie started to laugh, along with George and Price. 'Next thing, these two wogs started screaming at each other, and us, too, I think. I don't know what they were saying, we were too busy getting out of there. The last thing we saw as we drove off was them still screaming and crawling over the rubble with torches looking for their diving gear. The poor silly cunts.'

'Serves them right anyway,' said Price. 'Plundering the ocean's resources like that.'

'My sentiments exactly, Price,' agreed Norton, raising his glass.

'But of all the fuckin' times to get sprung by a couple of mugs.' Eddie shook his head and laughed. 'It was a bloody crack-up, when I look back on it.'

There was quiet for a moment, then Les spoke. 'So they're still in there. And now we've got to get them out?'

'Yes, unfortunately,' said George. 'Thanks to Waverley bloody Council.'

'And you've got a plan, have you, Eddie?' said Les.

'Yep. I sure have.' Eddie smiled and seemed to perk up. 'And it's a ripper.'

Les watched the little hitman rub his hands together and looked away. 'I hate it when you do that, Eddie,' he said.

Eddie continued to smile. 'Mate, it's all sweet. I got a bloke coming down with the explosives. We blow up the place. Grab the two bodies and throw them in a rubber ducky, which will come over from the boat-sheds. We transfer them to a game fishing boat, which another bloke'll bring around and have waiting for us.

He gets rid of them about twenty clicks out to sea. We take the rubber ducky back to the boatsheds. Leave it with the others. Then home to bed. Just in time for you to watch David Letterman.' Eddie winked at Les. 'Something like that anyway.'

'Something like that, eh?' Les looked at the evil glint in Eddie's eyes and shook his head. Underneath, Eddie loved all this shit.

'That's right.'

'And what about you, fat priest from the temple.' Les turned to George. 'Are you in on this, too.'

'You betcha, Rambo,' winked George. 'I wouldn't miss it for quids.'

Les turned back to Eddie. 'And who's this explosives expert you've got lined up?'

'This is where you're going to come in,' interjected Price. 'You're staying at some sheila's place, aren't you?'

'Yeah, but . . .'

'Well, that's where we'll put him.'

'What? Ohh, you're fuckin' kiddin'.'

'Well, it's better there than at your place,' reasoned Price.

'My place!!?' howled Norton. 'Who said anything about him staying at my joint in the first place?'

'Well, where else did you think we were gonna put him?' said Price. 'The Sebel bloody Town House? This is even better. No one'll see him round there.'

'Jesus, you cunts are good,' protested Les. He got up to get himself another drink. 'I'm supposed to be looking after a flat for an old friend, not holing up some IRA nutter. Or whatever he is.'

'Actually, he's an Australian,' said Eddie, his eyes following Norton as he got his drink and sat down again. 'Major Garrick Lewis. Ex-Army Intelligence. Special Ops. Shadow Company. And his nickname's The Gecko.'

'The Gecko,' repeated Les, sourly.

'That's him. You'll like him, too.'

'I suppose I'll bloody have to,' said Les.

'You'll pick him up at Central tomorrow,' said Eddie. 'He comes in on the 2.15 train from Newcastle.'

'What!!?' Despite having the shits, Norton burst out laughing. 'I pick him up from the 2.15 from Newcastle. What is this? Fuckin' *High Noon* or something? Give me a break, will you.'

'Look at the big sheila,' grinned George. 'He's cracking up under the pressure already.'

'Anyway,' Eddie rubbed his hands together again, 'that's all you need to know for the time being. I'll fill you in on any other details when The Gecko arrives tomorrow. We'll have a talk round Susie's place. In the meantime, why don't we just enjoy a nice drink? I feel like a few now.'

'Good idea,' agreed Billy.

Norton stared at the floor and shook his head. 'Yeah. Why bloody not.'

Price grinned and held up his glass. 'Cheers, Les,' he said. 'Shit! It's good to have you on the team.'

The team drank on with great gusto till all hours, swapping jokes, laughing about old times and present ones; and despite the shit that was about to go down, it wasn't a bad drink all round. There was no shortage of laughs in a boozy who-gives-a-stuff atmosphere. But when they all sobered up in the morning, each man knew it wasn't a picnic day at the beach they were planning and things could go wrong. Not to mention that the local constabulary frowned deeply upon people who blew up public or private property to remove bodies. Even if some of the said constabulary helped put some of the bodies there in the first place. They pulled up stumps around two, secured the club again and rang for two taxis; one to take George to Balmain, the other would drop the rest off at their various houses around the Eastern suburbs. The laughter in the second cab was a little subdued now, but they all managed to keep the bullshit going till Les got dropped off first. Have a good night's sleep, Les. Don't forget about tomorrow. Yeah, righto. I'll be in touch.

Somehow Norton managed to stumble through the front door, then into Susie's flat, and hit the correct security buttons. He fell out of his clothes, had a drink of water and cleaned his teeth and was feeling no pain when he fell onto Susie's bed. But Norton knew he would more than likely be feeling it in the morning, as well as remorse. So much for his quiet, laid-back week at Susie's, taping CDs. Now he'd have some ex-army mate of Eddie's staying with him. The galloping major. The galloping gecko'd probably be more like it. Norton yawned boozily and switched off the bedside lamp. Before long, Susie's map of the universe began to materialise on the bedroom wall. Les stared at it for a few moments, yawned boozily again, then laughed mirthlessly at this sudden and almost unexpected predicament. Ahh, who gives a stuff anyway. Next thing, Norton was lost in the cosmos again and snoring the sound sleep of the drunk; at times it almost sounded like the first stages of a Saturn rocket taking off.

Les had felt worse, but he'd also felt a lot better, when he surfaced around nine that morning and blundered from the bedroom to the bathroom, then into the kitchen. While he was standing there in his Speedos getting some coffee together, he figured he had about a warp five headache, so he blundered back into the bathroom, found what he was looking for and swallowed what he hoped would be enough to ease the nagging pain coming from somewhere in the middle of his head. After some fruit and cereal, toast and coffee, Norton felt at least good enough to start blundering through the day. The best thing to do, however, would be to have a run and sweat all the poisons and toxins out, then drink about a bucket of cold water. Les went into the lounge room and started putting on his Nikes while he thought about what he had to do today and what was going on. What *did* he have to do today and just what *was* going on again? Norton was probing through the boozy mists of his mind of last night at the club when the phone rang.

'Hello?'

'G'day, Les. It's Eddie. How are you?'

'I've been better.'

Eddie gave a bit of a chuckle. 'I know what you mean. Plenty of piss and a few laughs going round with the boys. It's a recipe for disaster.'

'Yeah,' agreed Norton. 'And it's lucky we don't have to do it too often.'

Eddie took Norton's subtle hint. 'Yeah, luckily.

Anyway, you know what you have to do today?'

Les nodded over the phone. 'Yeah. 2.15, Aunty Vera arrives. And I see that she gets here safe and sound.'

'That's it. I'll call round at three and we all might have a nice cup of tea. It'll be good to see Aunt Vera again.'

'You know where the place is?'

'Yeah. You gave it to me last night. Jesus, your handwriting's a bit rough when you're full of ink.'

'Eddie, I'm just on my way for a run. And I guarantee it's gonna be a lot fuckin' rougher than my handwriting.'

'I'll see you at three.'

'See you then, mate.'

Les looked at the phone for a moment, closed his eyes and shook his head reluctantly; what he would have preferred was another two hours of sleep. Instead, he laced up his Nikes, got into a pair of shorts, a T-shirt and sweatband, locked the flat up and walked outside, ready for about an hour of misery.

The wall of letterboxes opposite the corner where Macabee had been sitting was just high enough to do some easy stretches. Les limbered up for a few minutes and had his head down most of the time, so if any people walking past took any notice, he didn't see them. It wasn't a bad day; sunny with a few clouds around and a light nor'-easter. Norton didn't need any competition and he didn't need to do it too tough; just sweat all the piss out mainly. One lap of Royal Sydney Golf Course would do fine. It was nice and flat and not all that long, then a quick swim afterwards and dry off back at the flat. Les had one last stretch, touched his toes a couple of times, then trotted gingerly off down Hall Street. He turned left into Glenayr, left again at Curlewis, bolted across Old South Head Road before he got squashed by two trucks and about fifty cars full of impatient drivers, then jogged off easily alongside the Golf Links towards Newcastle Street. Before long, Les had gone past Rose Bay and was grinding up O'Sullivan Road, appreciating any shade from the trees along the golf links as the sweat poured down his face, stinging his eyes before it dripped off his chin onto his chest and arms. Then it was one more game of stuntman getting back across Old South Head Road, then back down Curlewis and across Campbell Parade before he pulled up at the bus stop near the start of Queen Elizabeth Drive.

After the run, Norton didn't know whether he felt better or worse; all he knew was he felt glad it was over. He had a long, cool drink of water while he soaked his head under the tap. That did feel better, and now for a swim. As he stood up, Norton's eyes were drawn towards Bondi baths which he'd been thinking about at times during his run. He had a quick glance at his watch and noticed he still had plenty of time. Why not go over and give the place a quick checkout before I have a swim? See just what's there. Plus it might be an idea if I show this major bloke that I at least know where the scene of the up-and-coming crime's going to be and I've got half an idea what's going on. Les wrung his sweatband out, had another drink of water and began walking down across the park towards the beach.

When he got to the promenade, Norton stopped at

the end of the railing for a few moments next to where a couple of kids had chained their bikes. Behind him a couple of surfers were using the shower, other people were walking past carrying boogie-boards or the ubiquitous plastic bottle of mineral water. The tide was fairly low, the sky and sea were both a crisp, bright blue. Seagulls hung in the air, tankers cruised past out towards the horizon, people were either scattered across the white sands or out in the surf, taking advantage of a few small swells rolling in. The nor'-easter had picked up, spreading a slight bump over the ocean, but it was still a picturesque day, showing Bondi Beach at its near best. Les took it all in for a short while, especially two girls in bright, if extremely brief, bikinis proceeding up the path leading to Notts Avenue.

The first thing that hit Les when he got to the steps, apart from a freak with a Walkman who wasn't watching where he was going, was a blast of thick, rancid air coming from the toilets, that made Les hold his breath. Ah, yes, you can't beat a nice smelly brasco for style. And what a delightful contrast. A view of Bondi's beautiful blue seas on one hand. And on the other, a smelly, rotten shithouse. Pooh! Les trotted up the steps, not letting his breath out until he reached Notts Avenue.

Walking towards the baths, Les noticed they looked clean and blue, but they were almost deserted; it would be lucky if there were six people between both pools. There was a sign on the wall, just under where the roof angles over towards the pool. BONDI PUBLIC BATHS. HOME OF THE BONDI ICEBERGS. VISITORS WELCOME. Beneath that, dangling forlornly over a brick balcony

near the door, was another sign. HANDS OFF THE ICE-
BERGS. HOME OF AUSTRALIAN WINTER SWIMMING SINCE
1929. The sign, like the rest of the place, had a hanging-
down look of defeat about it. As if 1929 had finally
caught up. Or vice versa. Yep, mused Les, looking at
the sign fluttering languidly in the breeze. I'll bet a lot
of water has flowed under the baths since then, so to
speak. And a lot of schooners flowed through the
Icebergs, too. Les strolled on past an alcove of Otto
bins, the fibro roof falling in over them and the locked
double glass doors of the club. A bit further on he
passed a yellow besser brick wall with a few strands of
rusty barbed wire on top, a locked high gate that evidently led to some caretaker's place and came out at
the park where Notts Avenue ended in a dead end and
a small park overlooking the ocean. There was a vacant
lot at the end of the wall and part of the handball court
jutted out below where the baths area finished. A narrow, sandy trail led through some scrubby bush and
weed down to the rocks and further on a set of steps
began where Notts Avenue ended, going down to a
pathway which meandered up to Mackenzies Point,
then round to Tamarama Beach.

Before he began climbing down the trail, Les peered
at what he could see of the handball court. Part of his
view was blocked by an old, ramshackle grey paling
fence at the end of the vacant lot which was full of rubbish. Hanging over the palings was a scrubby, flat tree
that looked like it was trying to push the entire fence
into the handball court below. Les could make out
some grimy besser brick wall and rusting cyclone wire,
but if the rest of the baths looked bad, this part looked

70

completely stuffed. He wiped some sweat from his eyes and started walking down.

The trail was just dirt, rubbish and dried scrub till it reached the rocks. Les clambered over the rocks for a few metres till he stood beneath the wall of the handball court where it sat facing out over the ocean under the caretaker's flat. A jump across a few more rocks brought Les to a locked gate dangling between two pumphouses and a sign saying TRESPASSERS PROSECUTED. PAY AT THE FRONT. A hop, step and a jump had Les up some more rocks and onto the top of one pumphouse, then up a short flight of faded blue and white stairs onto a long concrete landing. One way led past the pool to the entrance. The other went straight into the handball court. Les took a sharp left.

He entered through an alcove of grey or grimy yellow besser bricks and at first thought he might have walked into a handball court in Calcutta or maybe Jamaica. It was completely shitted out, mon. There was a covered area to his right of peeling yellow stucco and the first thing he noticed was a meter board saying JOHNSON PUMPS. NSW QLD WA. Above it a family of starlings had a nest and it was covered in streaks of brown, black and white shit. There was enough guano there to send Christmas Island broke. If that wasn't enough, there was another one in the corner that had copped the same amount of shit, or more from another nest. Running round the walls were the remains of a wooden bench and some wooden railings dotted with corroded metal clothes pegs. Most of the wooden railings were on the concrete floor next to the remains of old chairs, discarded clothes and other assorted rubbish rolling around in the dust and mud.

Les walked out into the handball court area. It was about thirty metres by thirty. One grey besser brick wall with a square hole in it faced the ocean, the wall behind the playing area was topped with twisted cyclone wire clinging to rusting poles and above the next wall was the grey picket fence that looked like it was ready to fall in at any moment and bring the scrubby tree with it. The handball court was green — mostly. What wasn't was chipped brown or cracks showing through the brick wall it was painted on. The white lines of the playing area showed and the battered metal plate, for low shots, still clung precariously to the far wall. But as far as a handball court went, you wouldn't hold the World Series there. Norton had a look round at the cyclone wire, the disgrace that passed for a wooden fence, plus the assorted rubbish everywhere, and shook his head. If the truth be known, we're doing them a favour blowing the place up. 1929? 1829'd be more like it. Blow it into 2099. Les walked over to the hole in the wall and gazed out again. This time he noticed a fair-sized rockpool beneath the handball court leading in from the ocean and on this side of the pool he also noticed a thick, rusty iron spike sticking out from the rocks which would be perfect for bringing a boat in; especially a rubber ducky. I'll bet that's where they'll tie up, he thought. Les walked back a pace or two and looked down at the granite, strengthened concrete floor. So that's roughly where they are, eh! Les jumped up and down on the concrete a couple of times. No disrespect meant there, fellahs. But I'm just wondering what the galloping

72

major's going to use to get through this? It'd want to be something good. Though they're not all that far down and that wall behind'd go like a pack of cards. Oh, well, Eddie said he was the best in the business. And that's enough for me.

Les had another look around and suddenly felt he was being watched. Or maybe it was just the thought he shouldn't have been in there in the first place, on top of not having paid his way in. Norton had seen enough anyway. He left the way he came — down the steps near the pumphouse, and the rocks by the gate, then more rocks past the rockpool. A wave had filled the pool and it just looked too blue and inviting. Ah! Who gives a shit? thought Les, and he plunged into the pool. It was sensational. The water was all bubbles and surge, like an open-air jacuzzi. Les dived up and down, wallowed around for a while then scrambled out over the rocks on the far side. Rather than get his wet Nikes full of dirt and dust climbing back up the trail, Les followed the rocks back to the steps and came up that way. He didn't seem to notice anyone around as he walked up to Notts Avenue. But Les still couldn't help feel that someone had been watching him. He stopped to adjust one of his socks just before where the yellow besser blocks started and had a last look over the rocks. A stocky fisherman casting out on the rocks past the pumphouse caught his eyes. That's not my big mate, the Russian fisherman, is it? Les had another look. I think it is. Can't see the other one, though. Les had another look round while he adjusted his sock again. Oh well. Feeling good after diving into the pool, Les soon got into his stride and squelched his way back up Hall Street to Susie's unit.

After a shower, some more water and another cup of coffee, Norton felt decidedly better than he had when he blundered out of bed earlier; there was no doubt the run and the swim did the trick. He was standing in the lounge room in a clean pair of jeans and a green Wallabies T-shirt taping one of Susie's Rippingtons CDs and thinking it was almost time he started heading for Central railway station when another thought struck him. When the galloping major got here, where was he going to sleep? He couldn't really expect him to doss on the lounge when there was a spare room. It was none of his business and Les wasn't all that interested, so he'd kept out of the boarder's room. Now it might at least be an idea to see what was in there. It was adjacent to Susie's and the door wasn't locked; Norton opened it and took his cup of coffee inside.

Ackerley's room was narrower than Susie's with a short, curtained window at the end that overlooked where the long, skinny balcony finished. There was a single wooden bed with drawers along the side and a built-in bedlamp in the far left corner and against the right wall was a skinny wardrobe with a small dressing table built onto its side. Next to the wardrobe were a couple of benches made out of milk crates with a number of books either standing up or falling over. A battered boogie-board and a pair of flippers lay against the wall on the left as you walked in and in the right corner there was an old barstool and desk on which a small word processor was sitting. The carpet was brown, the walls a kind of yellow, holding a couple of posters pinned with Blu-Tack — one of the original Star Trek crew, the other was some bloke sitting at a table in a suit and metal-framed glasses, smoking a pipe. Les had a closer look. Jean-Paul Sartre. Buggered if I know who that is, he shrugged. A thin black-and-white doona and matching sheets were crumpled across the unmade bed and there were four small rings in the dust on the shelf across the bedlamp where someone had removed a small radio.

Les put his coffee down on the desk, gave it and the beadstead a quick wipe with his hand, tidied the doona and straightened the pillow. That'll do you, major, nodded Les, picking up his coffee. On the way out he had a glance at a couple of books to gauge Ackerly's reading tastes. *Time Scale. An Atlas To The Fourth Dimension* by Nigel Calder. *The Cosmic Code. Quantum Physics and The Language of Nature* by Heina R. Pagels. Les put the books back and looked at one of the posters. Yes, beam me out, Scotty. He closed the door, switched off the stereo, rinsed his coffee cup in the sink, then locked up the flat and walked down to the garage.

Les managed to find a parking spot along the ramp that ran up past Belmore Park and he had a minute or two up his sleeve when he locked the old Ford and walked up to the Country Trains platforms. Now what did Eddie say again? You don't know him, but he knows you. Just stand under the big clock and Garrick will find you. Well, shrugged Les, a man can only do what a man's told to do. A minute or two later Les was doing exactly that — standing under the big clock, waiting. He stood there for a good ten minutes, watching the crowds of people around him coming and going, sitting, waiting, reading. Some carrying luggage, some not, some wearing Akubra hats or carrying guitars. Couples would embrace each other with happy greetings, other couples would be tenderly holding hands in a sad farewell. Les peered into the crowds of travellers or commuters trying to pick out someone that could be whoever it was he was supposed to meet. Maybe I've missed him, thought Les. Maybe he missed the train. Maybe I should light a cigarette, lean back against a wall like Marlene Dietrich in *The Blue Angel* and blow a stream of cigarette smoke up in the air. Norton kept looking about him and was thinking of getting an ice-cream when he heard a voice just to his left.

'Les Norton?'

Les turned slowly around. 'Yeah.'

'I'm Major Garrick Lewis. Eddie Salita said you were expecting me.'

It was hard to guess Major Lewis's age. He would have to have been at least in his fifties, but he looked more like a grainy mid-thirty, and the way he wore his brown hair wisped across his forehead in a kind of Beach Boys style gave him an even more youthful appearance. A pair of dark green eyes, set in a straight, square face above a slightly broken nose, seemed to weigh you up like a bag of tomatoes while he looked at you and a wide mouth stretched across two rows of perfect white teeth gave you the impression of a semi-permanent, if slightly cynical, smile. He was wearing plain light brown cotton trousers with a plain khaki shirt, a blue peak cap and a dark grey photographer's kind of vest with about a hundred different pockets in

76

it. There was a large, black, zipped-up canvas carry bag at his feet and an overnight bag across one shoulder. But what surprised Les was a metal crutch under his right arm. He had a white Adidas trainer on one foot and a sock on the other bound into a canvas and rubber brace or splint that went up to his shin. Great, thought Norton. The galloping major's a bloody cripple. And I'm lumbered with him.

'Yeah, that's right.' Norton offered his hand. 'I'm Les, anyway. Pleased to meet you — Major Lewis.'

'Call me Garrick. And I'm pleased to meet you too, Les.'

The major's handshake was brief, but very firm and very businesslike and when he straightened up off his crutch he came up to just under eye level with Les.

'The car's just out there,' said Les, nodding towards the main entrance. 'I'll give you a hand with your stuff.'

'Thanks, lad. I'd appreciate that.'

Norton picked up the major's bag and they started slowly towards the car. 'What happened to your ankle?'

'I sprained it.'

'I've done that,' replied Les. 'It's a proper bastard.'

'Yes,' agreed the major. 'It is.'

Les couldn't tell if Garrick was smiling when he said that or it just looked that way.

They didn't say anything else on the way to the car. Les put the major's bag in the back along with his overnight bag. He went to take Garrick's crutch but the major preferred to lay it in front of him after Les opened the door and he manoeuvred himself inside.

Norton climbed behind the wheel and they proceeded towards the Eastern suburbs. They went back up Eddy Avenue and had reached Albion Street without a word passing between them, when Les thought he'd better say something. He had the radio off and it was getting almost embarrassing.

'Well, I guess we both know what this is all about, Garrick.'

'Yes. Eddie's explained to me what's going on.'

'And did he tell you where you'd be staying?'

'Eddie explained all that, too,' replied the major.

'Right. Well at least we both know where we stand in that department.' They drove on in silence till they got to the Captain Cook Hotel.

'Did you, ah, have a good trip down?' asked Les. He didn't particularly care, but he had to say some bloody thing.

The major turned from the window to Norton. 'What exactly are you trying to say, Les? Is there something on your mind? Problems? Doubts?'

'No. No. Nothing like that.' Les shook his head. 'But I have to admit, I'm a bit curious about you. I mean, how do you know Eddie? What's your caper? I've been in a few capers with Eddie and Price.'

'Oh, don't worry, Les. I know all about you. I've even seen you in action. You're there, lad. No two ways about that.'

'That's very nice of you, Garrick. Now what about you. Where are you? Here, there, where? What about a bit of SP. Of course, if you don't want to tell me, that's okay. I understand. No offence, Major — sir.'

Major Lewis seemed to smile for a second. 'Okay,

Les. You want a full profile on Major Garrick W. Lewis, alias The Gecko. All right, I'll give it to you in a nutshell. I used to be in the army, I live on a farm on the North Coast with my wife and three kids, and I blow things up for a living.'

'That's it?' said Les.

'That, and I'm also what you could call a soldier of fortune. I was a major in the Australian Army. Army Intelligence. Special Operations. Then Shadow Company — where I met Eddie.' The major looked up at Les. 'I was an explosives expert, Les. More than that. I'm said to be the best there is. I was a scientist at Sydney University when I went straight into Army Intelligence and Special Ops. I can do things with explosives others are still thinking about.' Garrick smiled again and his tongue seemed to flick around his mouth, reminding Les somehow of a lizard. 'Now I just travel round the world blowing different things up for different people. Bougainville. Brunei. I did a lot of work during the Gulf War.'

'Bloody hell!' Norton was impressed. 'And you're married?'

'Yeah, married a Kiwi nurse I met in Vietnam. A Maori. So between my army pension and the odd explosion here and there, Les, I manage to feed the wife and kids, send them to school and keep a roof over our heads. And we all live happily on the farm.'

Norton had to smile. 'Well, bloody good onya, Garrick. Sounds like you've got it together. Good luck to you, mate.'

'Thanks, Les.' Lewis made a gesture with one hand. 'Of course, I have to admit I don't mind doing this on odd occasions. Life on the farm's good. But you need a bit of excitement now and again. Plus there's the earn, of course, Les.'

'Of course.'

'The wife knows what I do. She doesn't mind. Her and the kids are probably glad to get rid of me for a few days.'

'Do you like a drink, Garrick?

'Moderately.'

'Fair enough.' Les went past Bondi Junction towards Old South Head Road. 'Anyway, I imagine you and Eddie'll have a few things to talk about when you catch up with each other.'

'Yes. It'll be good to catch up with young Edward again.'

'Hey, Garrick. There was something else I wanted to ask you?'

'Yes, Les. What was that?'

'Eddie mentioned that same nickname you just did. The Gecko. How did you get it?'

Major Lewis rolled back the left sleeve of his shirt. Tattooed in black, brown, light blue and red on the inside of his forearm, was a fat gecko lizard, about ten inches long, with splayed tail and webbed fingertips. It looked good.

'So that's it,' said Les. 'It's a beauty.'

'That and something else,' said the Major.

'Something else?'

Garrick smiled and his tongue flicked across his lips. 'Yes. But we won't worry about that for the time being.'

Les nodded and thought he might let it go at that.

'Okay, Major — sir. Whatever you say. At ease or as you were. Take your pick.'

They headed down Old South Head Road to turn left into O'Brien. Garrick wasn't talking, which had Norton thinking. Yes, you can bet your life there's another side to Major Lewis. Alias The Gecko. Plenty he won't let on. Then why should he? And one thing was for sure. There's no shit in this bloke. He's the most straight up and down man I've met in a long while. He's a professional. He is a Soldier of Fortune. Les took a left at Simpson then a right into Hall. Though I wonder how the poor silly bludger stuffed his ankle? Next thing Les hit the buzzer, the shutter rolled up and they were in the garage. Les took Lewis' bag, helped him up the stairs and through the front door. Soon, Les had opened Susie's door, hit the security buttons and they were standing in the middle of the lounge.

The first thing Garrick said was, 'Shit! Look at all those bloody CDs.'

'Yeah,' said Norton. 'They belong to the owner. Come on, I'll show you your room.'

'Just hang on a minute, Les.' Garrick placed his crutch on the lounge, sat down next to it and began unlacing the canvas splint round his ankle. Les watched as he finally got it off, tossed it to one side and started rubbing and scratching his foot. 'Ohh, shit! You reckon that doesn't feel better.'

With a kind of dry look on his face, Les watched Lewis stand up, walk round the flat and do a few squats. You didn't have to be an orthopaedic surgeon to see there was nothing wrong with his ankle. 'That's an amazing cure, Garrick. How did you do it? The power of prayer?'

'Exactly, Les.' The Gecko smiled back from over near the curtains. 'All the way down in the train, I prayed that my ankle would get better. And it has. It's a miracle, Les.'

'Yeah,' nodded Norton. 'You should be working with Tammy Baker. And I just rolled into town on a cabbage. Don't give me the shits.'

The Gecko sat back down on the lounge, picked up his crutch and stood it in front of him. 'Les, would you do me a favour, please? Would you put my crutch against the wall.' He pushed his crutch over to Norton.

Les went to catch the crutch easily, expecting just a light alloy frame. Instead, it was that heavy it forced his arm back and he almost dropped it. Norton held it for a moment, then looked at Garrick. 'What the . . .?'

'Parts of spent uranium shells from the Gulf War, Les. Heavy little critters, aren't they. Try lugging them on and off a train all day stuffed inside a lead-lined crutch.'

Les looked a bit gingerly at the crutch he was holding in his hand. 'Spent uranium shells?'

'Yes. The American Tank Divisions used them as tips for their anti-tank shells. I've got pieces of them in there and I know how to cook them up again.'

'Cook them up again?' Norton's eyes were like ping-pong balls when he stared at The Gecko. 'You're not going to . . .'

Garrick laughed and shook his head. 'No, Les. Nothing like that. I'm just going to make a low-yield fusion thing. Normally this is for smashing through solid metal. Concrete'll be like a piece of sponge cake.

And nice and neat.' The Gecko stretched his arms. 'There'll be a little bit of radioactivity. But nothing to worry about.'

'Nothing to worry about,' repeated Norton.

The Gecko shook his head and a few strands of brown hair wisped across his forehead. 'No, nothing really. Now,' he said, rising to his feet, 'which is my room, lad?'

Even though he knew Major Lewis wasn't a cripple, Les picked up his bags for him. 'In here, mate.'

Garrick said he wanted to unpack a few things and sort some others out. He didn't say anything about the room. He just picked up his crutch and put it carefully in one corner. Les showed him where the phone was and the bathroom, closed the door and left Major Lewis to his own devices. If he wanted him, he'd be in the kitchen. Les made coffee for one, then sat down and had another think before Eddie arrived.

Well, isn't this a nice kettle of fish I've got myself into. Or crutch full of uranium. That bloke might be a soldier of fortune, but half the seats are missing off his Ferris wheel. What's he gonna do? Melt the concrete with low-yield fusion, or some bloody thing? Great. won't that be a nice blow-up, so to speak, if it goes wrong. Norton shook his head while he sipped his coffee. Still, I suppose it couldn't be any worse than that silly bloody thing me and Murray let off back home. Bloody Eddie. He sure knows how to find them. But how the hell do I get mixed up in all this shit? All I was doing was helping out an old friend in her moment of need. I was on a bloody good thing. Les shook his head again. Still, it's only till Friday — with a bit of luck.

Les heard the shower run and stared disconsolately into his coffee and wondered how all this shit he didn't want to be in in the first place would pan out. He was still staring into his coffee, after the shower stopped, when the intercom buzzed. Les got up and walked over to the sink.

'Hello. Eisenberg bar-mitzvah.'

'It's Rabbi Goldman. Open the door, I got some good tips for you.'

Les zapped the front door, then let Eddie into the kitchen. The little hitman was wearing jeans and a T-shirt, much like Les.

'So how's it going, Eddie. All right?'

'Good. Yeah. Lewis get here okay?'

'Yeah. He's just got out of the shower. You want a coffee?'

'Glass of cold water?'

'In the fridge,' replied Les, sitting back down at the kitchen table. 'Help yourself.'

Eddie found a glass and opened the fridge. 'So how have you found Major Garrick Lewis?'

'Surprising,' replied Norton. 'Very surprising.'

Eddie sat down with his glass of water. 'So you both got on all right?'

'Like two little lovebirds,' smiled Les.

Eddie detected just a hint of sarcasm in Norton's voice. 'What did he say to you?'

Norton leant across the table. 'Eddie, who does this cunt think he is? Frederick fuckin' Forsyth? He's gonna blow the bloody joint up with spent uranium shells, or some fuckin' thing, from the Gulf War.'

Eddie eased back, smiled and made an open-handed

gesture. 'I told you he was the best. And talking about the best . . .' Eddie looked up.

'Hello, young Edward,' came a voice from near the kitchen door.

'Gecko!' Eddie's face broke into a grin. He got up, then walked over and shook Garrick's hand. Les watched as they went into the usual backslapping and bonhomie two old friends are apt to do when they catch up with each other after a while.

'Jesus! You're looking well, Eddie.'

'So are you. But,' Eddie made another gesture with his hands, 'when didn't you?'

Lewis was wearing boxer shorts and a plain white T-shirt. He had strong legs, a flat stomach, hard sinewy arms and equally strong-looking hands. Norton had to agree. 'Can I get you something, Garrick. Coffee, tea . . .?'

Garrick moved into the kitchen, looked at Norton's plunger and took a sniff. 'That coffee looks all right. Any chance of one?'

'I'll make a fresh pot.'

'Yeah, bugger it, I'll have a coffee too,' said Eddie.

'Susie's got some nice Vienna shortbreads there with chocolate cream,' said Les, another hint of sarcasm in his voice. 'I can arrange a plate of them for you, too.'

'Good idea,' nodded Eddie. 'Bring them into the lounge room. We'll be in there.'

Eddie and Major Lewis went inside and sat on the lounge; Les could hear them laughing while he got the coffee and that together. They should give me a little maid's outfit, he smiled to himself, as he opened the packet of biscuits. Norton found a tray, put the coffee and everything on it, then took it into the lounge room and placed it on one of Susie's coffee tables while he pulled up a lounge chair.

'Ahh, good on you, Les. You're a beauty,' said Eddie.

'Thank you very much, Les,' said Garrick politely. 'That looks good.'

'No trouble, mate.'

Eddie and The Gecko poured themselves a coffee, as did Les, and then they settled back and began picking at the biscuits. For three hard men about to discuss, then commit, a fairly serious crime, it was all very cosy.

'So you've met Garrick,' Eddie said to Norton.

'Yep,' nodded Les.

'And you remember when I told you he was the best in the business?'

'Yep,' Les nodded again.

Eddie turned to his old army mate. 'Well, tell Les some of your little tricks, Gecko. Tell him about the bloke with the toothbrush.'

Major Lewis gave his shoulders a shrug. 'Why don't you tell him, Eddie. You've always been better at telling stories then me.'

'Back in Vietnam, Les. We had to get rid of different people on odd occasions. North Vietnamese cadres. ARVN generals. The odd American officer now and again when they went a bit loopy. We had to knock this cadre for . . . for whatever. Anyway, I was gonna shoot him. But The Gecko says no. We'll blow him up. I'll put a bomb in his toothbrush. So he sets a bomb in his toothbrush that worked on saliva. As soon as the poor mug put it in his mouth, it blew his head completely off. It was hilarious.'

'It's amazing the amount of germs you find in saliva,' nodded The Gecko.

Les shook his head in mild admiration and sipped his coffee.

'And what about the bloke with the typewriter,' said Eddie, rocking around on the lounge. 'Les, he set a bomb in this bloke's typewriter. It was a Yank colonel who'd cracked up and was getting everyone in the shit. The bloke always used to end his letters "I remain as always". So the Gecko set the thing to go off as soon as he hit those keys in that order. The poor prick's gone to finish this letter and bingo! He got blown into sushi. It was beautiful.'

'Actually, I packed just a bit too much in,' said Garrick. 'And there was a little collateral damage that time.'

'Only that young Vietnamese poof he was humping.' Eddie rocked around on the lounge again. 'At least they died together as lovers.'

'Yeah. They certainly remained as always,' smiled The Gecko.

Eddie was still bouncing around on the lounge. 'But what about the letter bomb.'

'Letter bomb?' echoed Les.

'Yeah. We were going to send this Yank general a letter bomb. But The Gecko says, fuck sending him a letter bomb, we'll send him a postcard bomb.'

'A postcard bomb?' Norton screwed his face up. 'That's impossible. Unless you put it in an envelope.

And people hardly ever put postcards in envelopes. That's the idea of them,' he shrugged.

'Exactly, Les,' said Eddie. 'Tell him what you did, Garrick.'

The Gecko smiled and licked his lips. 'I got his fingerprints and his DNA and impregnated them onto this thin sheet of liquid crystal inside the postcard and the photo on the front. I rigged it so that when his and only his fingerprints made contact with the front of the postcard it set off a reaction and whammo! Not enough to kill him, but enough to blow his fingers off and blind him in one eye. And enough to get the prick out of the war before he got any more poor people killed for nothing.'

Norton shook his head again. This time he was impressed. Impressed not only at The Gecko's expertise in his field, but at meeting a full-on assassin. A soldier of fortune. Les always knew Eddie was a killer and Les had killed under different circumstances. But Major Garrick Lewis was something again. Killing didn't seem to worry him in the least. He found it a challenge, then sort of analysed it and half-joked about it. And when he was out to get you, you literally wouldn't know what hit you, till it hit you. As well as being impressed, Norton thought he might ease up on the jokes too. If I give this bloke too much cheek he's likely to set a bomb in my brasco paper. One wipe and zappo! Kiss your arse goodbye.

'Well, you certainly sound as if you know what you're doing, Garrick,' said Les.

The Gecko sipped his coffee. 'Yeah, I got half an idea what's going on.' He turned to Eddie. 'Now about that . . . what I wanted to discuss with you.'

'Yeah. Well . . . umh.'

Although they weren't looking at him when they spoke, Les knew pretty much what and who they were talking about and quickly got the hint. 'Listen, I imagine you two villains have got a million things you want to talk about, so go for your life. I was going to tape some of Susie's CDs and I can do it with the headphones on.' Before Eddie and Garrick knew what was going on, Norton had torn the cover off another cassette, had Susie's headphones round his neck and explained exactly what he was about to do. 'I'm not missing out on a chance to tape the best of these CDs,' he concluded, 'bombs or no bombs.'

'Fair enough, Les,' said Eddie. 'Good idea.' He ran his eyes over the table full of CDs. 'Christ! Hasn't she got some.'

Les winked at The Gecko, who smiled back, then picked out five CDs and filled the stacker. The two men on the lounge got into talking about whatever, and Les started flicking through the James Harman Band's 'Do Not Disturb'. Oh yes, Norton smiled to himself. 'I'm Gone' and 'Icepick's Confession'. Aren't they a couple of good tracks. Before long, Les had Bob Margolin's 'Boogie At Midnight'. Anson Funderburgh and The Rockets' 'A Man Needs His Loving' and 'Red Hot' by Lee Roy Parnell all taped, plus a heap of other tracks that took his fancy. He even found 'Trailer Load of Guns' by Jnr Cat amongst Susie's reggae collection and taped it too. As well as being a good track it reminded Les of his seedy hotel room in Montego Bay and the people he met while he was in Jamaica. Norton couldn't hear a word Eddie and Major Lewis were saying so he didn't pay them much attention. But one minute they'd be laughing and bouncing all over the lounge, the next minute they'd be deadly serious.

Garrick took Eddie into the bedroom and showed him the special crutch, then they came out, sat on the lounge, looked at some photos and got into more serious discussion. Les had one tape finished and was into another when he felt a tap on his shoulder. It was Eddie. Les removed the headphones.

'I'm going to get going.'

'Okay.' Les put the headphones on the floor and stood up. 'So . . .?'

'We've gone over the whole thing from top to bottom. Garrick'll fill you in on everything. So from now on, you just look after him and see that he gets it all together.'

'Fair enough,' agreed Les.

'And this is from Price for food and if you have to do any running around or that.' Eddie handed Les a thousand dollars. 'He reckons if you do the catering, Garrick'll be eating out of the Otto bins at the back of McDonald's.'

'Tell him thanks.' Les gave Eddie a wry smile and put the money in his pocket. 'So you'll ring — or what?'

'Yeah. I'll be in touch. Billy'll look after the club for the next three nights and give them the same electrical fault spiel. Price didn't want to close the club completely, just in case.'

'Of course,' nodded Les. 'Plus he and George can sit on their arses in comfort, while we go out and blow ours up.'

'Exactly,' agreed Eddie. 'Do you blame them?'

Norton shook his head. 'No.'

Eddie moved towards the door. 'It's not much use us being seen together. So I'll ring you. Then I'll see you on the day. Then on the night. 10.00 p.m.'

'Then I catch the 11.37 back to Newcastle,' said Major Lewis.

'The 11.37? Shit! That's cutting it a bit fine,' said Norton.

'That's the way I've planned it,' replied The Gecko.

'Fair enough,' answered Les.

'Anyway, I'm out of here,' said Eddie.

The Gecko stood up, he and Eddie shook hands again and said goodbye, then Eddie was gone. When he went out the front door he gave the intercom a couple of quick buzzes as he went past. The Gecko sat back down on the lounge and kind of stared and smiled at Les; as if he was thinking about something and taking him in at the same time. Norton sat down on the footstool near the phone.

'He's a character — Eddie,' said Norton.

'Yes, he certainly is,' agreed The Gecko. 'We had some times together, I can assure you. And you probably don't need me to tell you this, but he's one of the best there is, too. He saved my neck a couple of times.'

'I'd believe that,' nodded Les. 'We've had a few times together, too. Anyway, what do you want to do? You hungry or something? Maybe you'd like to go for a bit of a stroll, now that your ankle's come good.'

'The power of prayer, eh?' smiled The Gecko. 'No. I didn't think you'd quite fall for that one, Les Norton.' Major Lewis looked directly at Norton for a few moments;

91

still thinking and still taking him in. 'No,' he said slowly, 'You know where I'd like to go right now, Les?'

'Down the handball court at the back of The 'Bergs?'

'Exactly.'

'I thought you might. You'll need a good pair of trainers or something. We've got to climb over a lot of rocks covered in barnacles and shit.'

'Good lad,' nodded The Gecko, continuing to smile his lizard smile at Les. 'I'll get changed.'

Ten minutes later they walked out the front door. Major Lewis was wearing a plain grey tracksuit, the same cap, Brooks basketball boots and he was carrying his overnight bag. When they got to the front of the flats, Macabee was sitting in his usual place, playing his twin roles of concerned citizen and local nark.

'G'day, boss,' said Les, a little cheekily. 'How's things. Seen your two mates, the Chibi fishermen?'

'Caichibi bastards,' replied Macabee, and he spat on the ground.

'My sentiments exactly,' replied Norton.

'What did that old bloke just say?' asked Major Lewis, sounding a little inquisitive.

'Buggered if I know,' said Les. 'He's dirty on these two Russian blokes that are staying here.'

'Russians?'

'Yeah. You'll probably see them around. They do a bit of fishing.'

'Mmmhh.' The Gecko turned round for another look at Macabee and they continued on their way.

Rather than walk down Hall Street, where there was a chance he might bump into someone he knew, Les cut into Jacques Avenue, then straight down Lamrock, across Campbell Parade and down Notts Avenue. The wind was coming from the south now with quite a few clouds around. There were a few people on the beach or out surfing, but the baths were completely deserted. The only sign of life was the 'Hands Off The 'Bergs' sign flapping languidly in the late afternoon breeze. That and the odd jogger or power walker, or dog owner taking his or her dog for a crap somewhere so the joggers and power walkers could step in it. The Gecko gave the baths a bit of a once-over as they walked past, then they were standing where the baths ended, staring down the vacant lot at the old wooden fence clinging desperately above the end of the handball court.

'Christ!' said The Gecko. 'Who's their carpenter? That's in worse shape than the rest of the joint.'

'I think he died in 1930. A year after the place opened.'

Major Lewis shook his head, then noticed the trail winding down to the rocks. 'This is where we go down?'

'Yeah. Follow me. You just have to watch the rocks at the bottom.'

Les started down the trail with the major about two metres behind him. There was a bit of bump running when they got to the rocks and the rockpool had filled up, so you had to watch the swells as well as your footing or if you didn't go on your backside you'd at least get a good soaking. Les judged the waves carefully then hopped, stepped and jumped his way over and up to the steel gate between the two pumphouses. The Gecko arrived on his heels and not puffing one bit. Norton had an instinctive look around. There wasn't a soul in sight, so they climbed up the rocks and the steps, then took a left straight into the handball court, stopping near the peeling brick columns holding up the concrete shelter.

'Christ!' said The Gecko, looking around him. 'What a shit fight. Have a look at that bloody fence.' He walked over to the handball court, then back to Les inside the sheltered part. 'Bloody hell!' he muttered, looking at the bird shit. 'I wouldn't mind having the guano contract on the place.' There was a small wooden door Les hadn't noticed before, built up from the floor and into the wall. Garrick opened it and got a blast of sour, mildewed air coming from the rubbish, slime and filthy water inside. He quickly slammed it and pointed to some brown stains running down the walls above their heads. 'God! Have a look at the rust coming out of the walls. That's all the iron supports in the foundations rusting away.' Major Lewis had another look around and shook his head in disgust. 'This place is a fuckin' disgrace. It's absolutely filthy.'

'You trying to say you wouldn't have it in your regiment, Major?'

'My regiment?' The major snorted some air out of his nostrils. 'We're doing them a favour blowing the dump up.'

Les nodded and smiled. 'That's exactly what I said when I first saw the joint.'

'The thing is, though,' said the major, slowly picking at his chin, 'I might need to be a bit more careful than I thought. Too much and the whole bloody she-mozzle might go.'

Norton's smile disappeared and he got a sudden, awful feeling in the pit of his stomach. I knew it. I just bloody knew it.

'Though the floor here doesn't seem to be in too bad a condition,' said Garrick, banging his foot on the ground out from the shelter a couple of times. 'Anyway, only one way to find out.' The Gecko put his overnight bag on the ground and began to unzip it. 'You can . . . stand at ease, Les.'

'Thank you, Major — sir.' Les smiled, threw the major half a salute then leant up against the brick columns supporting the shelter.

Major Lewis pulled a black plastic and metal device from his overnight bag, about the same size as a school-kid's pencil case. It had a kind of small aerial at one end, a screen and a number of buttons and switches. He flicked a switch on the side; the screen lit up in blue and a thin shaft of red light came from the aerial. Les had seen something like it before: a laser pointer. But he imagined this one would be for calculating depth and dimensions and probably just about everything else.

Garrick began pointing it around and pressing different buttons while he wrote down different numbers and calculations on a small pad. He walked up and down the whole area, looked out the hole in the wall a few times, even checked out the caretaker's unit above. But mainly he moved the device around where the bodies were buried in a very careful grid pattern, stopping now and again as if he was concerned about something. Norton didn't have much of a clue as to what he was doing, but it was beautiful just standing there watching a genius at work. After a while The

Gecko gave the area a grudging nod of approval, switched the device off, then walked over to where Les was standing and put it back in his overnight bag along with the writing pad.

'Well, I can't see any real problems, Les,' he said, dragging the 'real' out a little.

'Any *reealll* problems,' echoed Norton.

'That old fence and the wall up there. They'll more than likely come down. But they should land in that far corner, along with the tree. And that wall there.' Garrick pointed to the wall overlooking the ocean with the hole it. 'That'll go. So I'm thinking there'll be besser bricks and shit all over the rocks below, which could make it a bit tricky scrambling down there in the dark, dragging two bodies.'

'You could sprain an ankle if you're not careful.'

Major Lewis stared directly at Norton. 'Exactly, Les. Exactly. However, the force and heat of the explosion should cauterise a lot of it together, possibly giving us a smooth passage.'

'And blowing out all this concrete and shit underneath us. That's all sweet?'

The Gecko nodded slowly towards the floor. 'Yeah. It's a little thicker than I thought. But I've made several soundings and gone over my calculations thoroughly. So it shouldn't be any problem. The blast plus the heat will layer that off out into the ocean and it should end up looking like a billiard table underneath. We'll dig them out easy. It'll be a piece of cake, Les.'

'A piece of cake,' repeated Norton.

The Gecko looked from the concrete floor up at Les. 'Eddie *did* say two bodies — didn't he?'

'Yeah. A boxer and some cop. Why?'

Major Lewis shook his head. 'Oh nothing, Les. Nothing.'

Norton shrugged his shoulders. 'Anyway, Garrick, all that coffee's gone through me. I got to have a leak.'

'Yes, not a bad idea,' agreed Major Lewis. 'I could do with one myself.'

'What about underneath those two wall boxes with the bird shit all over them,' suggested Norton. 'Give it an extra ambience.'

'Sounds good to me.'

Les unzipped his fly, The Gecko pulled down the front of his tracksuit pants, then they chose a cabinet each and began piddling away. Les was enjoying the relief of a good pee and nonchalantly watching the stream of froth and yellow water near his feet, making sure he didn't step in it, when he casually glanced over at Major Lewis to see how he was going. Norton gave a double, triple blink. At first he thought the major was standing there pissing with one knee up. But no, circumcised, with a great, big purple head on it like an eggplant, was the biggest dick Les had ever seen. It was hard to tell its exact width and length. But it was a monster. Bloody hell! thought Les. If I owned that I'd put a shoe on it and make it do its own walking. Shit! The major was casually pissing away, no hands, his dick sitting on the top of his tracksuit pants, when Norton's eyes narrowed and he had a closer look. Tattooed down one side was another gecko in the same colours as the one tattooed on his arm. Norton chuckled to himself. Now I know the other reason you got that nickname 'The Gecko', Major. Christ! I wonder what that gecko ends up looking like when he gets that thing going. One of those giant dragon lizards they got in Borneo. Les shook his head in admiration. Well, hats off to you again, Major Lewis. You never fail to impress. And one thing's for sure, you'll never get charged with rape having a cock like that. It'd be assault with a deadly weapon. Norton zipped up his fly and turned around to find the major had finished too.

'Well, what do you want to do now, Garrick? You got enough info here?'

The major nodded. 'Yes. I might come back down again tomorrow. If not, I'll just do it Friday night as planned.'

'Okay, we might as well get going then.'

'I wouldn't mind a bite to eat soon. I'm getting a bit peckish. How about you, Les?'

'Good idea. We'll go home and get cleaned up a bit first. Then I'll take you somewhere decent.'

'Sounds good to me,' replied Major Lewis, picking up his overnight bag. 'Let's go.'

They left the way they came; down the steps then hop, step and jumping across the rocks. The southerly caught a bigger wave, hitting the rocks, so they both copped some spray and got their clothing a little wet. But it was no big deal. If anything, it was a bit of a buzz and the cool sea spray was both bracing and refreshing. Like Les did earlier, they avoided the sandy trail, preferring to take the steps at the end of Notts Avenue.

As they went past the vacant lot, Major Lewis spoke. 'Les, you know when we were in the handball court having a leak?'

'Yeah,' grunted Norton.

'Well, I had this feeling someone was watching me.'

Les coloured a bit. He wasn't sure what the major was on about and whether he was having a bit of a go at him for staring at his massive tool. 'No,' replied Norton, shaking his head adamantly, 'I didn't see anybody around.'

'Mmmhh. I just had this feeling someone was watching me.'

Les still wasn't sure if the major was having a bit of a go at him, but there was a certain tone in his voice. 'To tell you the truth, though, I got the same feeling when I was down here earlier. But I think it was one of those two Russian fishermen I was telling you about.'

'What do they look like, Les?'

Norton shrugged. 'One's a big bloke. Big chest, grey hair. The other's younger. Fitter, kind of lean-looking.'

'Dark, gaunt kind of face. Malevolent, sort of?'

'Yeah, I s'pose you could say that, Garrick. Why?'

'Oh, nothing, Les. Nothing.' The Gecko smiled and his tongue flicked over his lips. 'Come on. Let's get back to the flat. That quick burst of sea air has put quite an edge on my appetite.'

'Yeah, me too.'

They continued up Notts Avenue and headed towards Lamrock.

Back at the flat, the major said he wanted to get changed, then check a few of his calculations while they were fresh in his mind; he said he'd be about thirty minutes. This suited Les. He had a shave in Susie's en suite, then changed into a blue Australian

Surfer Headquarters T-shirt and got a beer from the fridge. He sipped it in the lounge room while he fiddled around, taping a few more tracks from the seemingly inexhaustible supply of CDs.

Les was tapping his foot to an old James Brown number, 'Too Funky In Here', when The Gecko came out, closing the bedroom door behind him. He was wearing the same trousers as earlier with a short-sleeved blue denim shirt, minus the vest and cap. Les turned the stereo right down and smiled.

'So how'd you go, Garrick? Everything looking all right?'

Major Lewis nodded. 'Yes, as good as gold.'

'Okay, then what say we go and have a bite to eat.'

'That sounds like a good idea to me, Les.'

'We'll go over to the Hakoah Soccer Club. It's only about two minutes from here and I'm a member. The food's real good. Go for the roast veal and vegies. They serve it with this creamed spinach you'd kill for.'

The Gecko nodded his head again. 'I can relate to that, Les. I've had to kill people over food before.'

Norton finished his bottle of beer and dropped the empty in the kitchen tidy. Yes, I can relate to that. He switched off the stereo, hit the security buttons and they headed for the Hakoah.

By the time they got there and Les had signed Garrick in, they'd managed to miss the screaming hordes in the restaurant getting into the $4 specials. So it was fairly civilised as they pushed their trays along the rail and filled their plates with roast veal, vegies, creamed spinach, Waldorf salad, pasta salads, beetroot with horseradish, and all sorts of other tasty things

100

from the salad bar, plus beautiful, fresh bread rolls and bottles of mineral water. Les paid and they settled down at a table near the stairs, Les with his back to the front entrance. As they were eating, Les glanced over to where he'd been sitting the time he bumped Kelvin Kramer in the club. That caper with KK ended up involving nuclear weapons and he hoped this wasn't some sort of weird coincidence. Whatever Norton's thoughts, the food in front of him soon shifted them to the back of his mind; it was delicious. The major wasn't quite as good on the tooth as Les. But when Norton went over and got two coffees, The Gecko came back big on the bread rolls. He spread several thick with butter and monstered them one after the other.

'Well, what did you think, Garrick?' asked Norton. 'Good food?'

'Delicious, Les,' smiled the major. 'An excellent choice. Thank you for bringing me here.'

Les shrugged. 'It was a pleasure, mate.' Norton was pleased he'd brought the major somewhere good. He was a strange bloke in a way; especially with that cynical kind of smile. But for some reason, making The Gecko happy made Les happy. 'Your wife a good cook, Garrick?' Norton asked, looking over the top of his coffee. 'What's she like in the kitchen?'

'Pretty good,' enthused the major. 'Her father's Spanish. So we get lots of paellas and things. If you've ever watched "Floyd On The Mediterranean". Well, whatever he cooks, we get.'

Les gave a grudging nod of approval. 'You could do a lot worse than that, mate.'

The Gecko settled into his seat and looked evenly at

Les for a few moments, his piercing green eyes seeming to take everything in. He had that odd lizard smile on his face that still kept throwing Norton off. When he was smiling, it looked almost like he wasn't. And when he wasn't, it somehow looked like he was.

'Did I ever tell you how I met my wife, Les?' he said casually.

Les kind of nodded and shook his head at the same time. 'You said something about Vietnam.'

'That's right.' The major eased a little closer over the table. 'You see, Les. I like really rough sheilas.'

'Rough?' Norton wasn't quite sure how to take this. Was the major a trifle bent? Or was it because of his monster donger that was all he could get?

'Yeah, Les. The rougher and more horrible the better. I met her at a party in Bien Hoa. A nurses' party. I walked in, got full of ink and said to the sheila running the show, point me out the roughest, most uncouth nurse in the place. And she introduced me to Quireda. So I got her pissed on rum, dragged her back to my quarters and ripped all her clothes straight off, which she copped sweet. So while she was standing there with no gear on. I got a cigar out of my drawer and a box of those American wax matches. I stuck the cigar in my mouth, struck the match on her tits, lit it and blew a big cloud of smoke in her face.'

'Shit! What did she say?'

'Nothing. Not a word. So I started getting my gear off to give her one. When I turned around though, she was standing there, bent over, the cheeks of her arse spread apart and her date stuck up in the air. I said to her. What are you doing? And you know what she said, Les?'

'No, Garrick. What did she say?'

'She said, "I just thought you might like to open a couple of bottles of beer before we get started." Now how are you not going to fall in love with a woman like that?'

'Yeah,' nodded Les dumbly. 'I . . . suppose it'd be pretty hard not to.'

The Gecko's green eyes never left Norton's. 'But even though I'm happily married. I still get a stray root if I want one.'

'You do?'

The Gecko nodded. 'My sister-in-law lives on the farm and she's got a glass eye. She takes it out and lets me root her in the socket.'

'Ohh, come on, Garrick. Give me a break. That's awful.'

'Hey! Don't knock it,' enthused Major Lewis. 'It's one of the best roots I've ever had.'

Norton shook his head. 'No, count me out.'

'All right. But I'm telling you, Les, it's the grouse. It's better than any root or blow job I've ever had. You should come up some time and give it a go.'

Norton shook his head again. 'No, I'm pretty right, thanks.'

The Gecko gave a bit of a shrug. 'Oh well, please yourself. But if ever you change your mind, let me know when you're coming and I'll tell my sister-in-law to keep an eye out for you.' Major Lewis stood up. 'Toilets over there, Les?'

'Yeah, just down to the right.'

'Thanks. That bloody coffee does go through you, doesn't it.'

During the major's absence Les sat and stared into his coffee. He didn't know whether to laugh, cry or just bang his head on the table. The Gecko had him completely flummoxed. He just never ceased to amaze. And if he'd only get that smile off his face when they were together, so Les could tell where he was coming from now and again.

The major returned, sat down and took a sip of coffee, then started picking at another bread roll.

'So what do you fancy doing now, Garrick?' asked Les. 'You want to go home and watch a bit of TV or . . .'

'To be honest, Les, I wouldn't mind going for just a couple of quiet drinks. Not a pub or a club. Something different. You know a quiet bar round here?'

'Actually I do know a place we can go.'

'Yeah? Whereabouts?'

'Just down the beachfront. It's called Redwoods. Come on, I'll tell you about it on the way down.'

'Okay.' The major followed Les out the front doors of the club, then down Hall Street.

Redwoods had only been open about a month or so and Les had been a fairly regular customer since almost the first week. It was in Campbell Parade near the old Biltmore Hotel, about two doors from where some builders were currently renovating an old block of flats. Norton happened to be walking past one afternoon and a couple of blokes he knew were sitting just inside, so he joined them for a few cool ones and had been going back ever since. The place seemed to have something about it. Two removable sliding glass doors stood just above the footpath and inside was all solid wooden furniture, wooden floors and cream-coloured stucco walls dotted with round decals of various sizes that looked something like old Aztec calendars. A long, L-shaped bar angled out from the wall on the right as you entered and ran down to a couple of steps leading to the toilets, the kitchen and another two eating areas out the back. The bar was more solid wood, with seating for about fifteen, and started under a glass cabinet holding a couple of Redwoods T-shirts and finished at the coffee machine. Behind this was a door which led to a fire escape and a storage area. The bar was well stocked with shelves full of liquor and was split by a large, solid wooden cupboard crammed with more liquor; the staff had pinned different banknotes to the shelves and placed a fluffy, brown muppet doll on the end of one. Speakers in the corners played easy rock, fans hummed languidly from the ceiling and, besides the soft restaurant lighting, several pinpoints of light hung over the bar, giving Redwoods a pleasant and extra touch of atmosphere.

The drinks were always good, the service friendly and the food was tops. You could get anything from a Cajun chicken burger with tabouli, yoghurt and tomato relish, to a grilled sirloin with onion chutney and wedges, to a mixed board of sushi, to tomato and bocconcini salad with basil and rocket. Another thing Les liked about Redwoods was the doorman. He was a big, black American called Jee. Jee was built like a linebacker or something for the LA Rams, with close-cropped hair, but he had a huge infectious white smile that was almost as big as he was. Everybody liked him and he had the knack of making everybody feel welcome; especially Les. The owner was a different kettle of fish — a tall, rangy bloke with dark hair and a broken nose, who everybody called Marty. The rumour was, Marty was a helicopter pilot and made a bundle flying choppers during the Gulf War, which was how he bought the restaurant. Les thought it was a good story; though at over six feet four he just couldn't picture Marty leaping in and out of helicopters in a hurry.

But the bar was always full of nice enough people and interesting characters and somehow or other, through Jee or the owner, Les got to meet a few of them. He was at the bar one night and Kylie Minogue ordered a drink almost next to him. James Packer would come in and have a meal with his girlfriend. Virginia Hey, James Reyne or Vince Sorrenti would have a drink or a meal there. Different actors, authors, film directors, models, boxing promoters, etc, would drift in from time to time. Definitely not your 'pie and schooners' mob from the local boozer, yet there was no posing in the place and nobody tried to bung on any side. It was just a good place to have a meal and a drink.

Norton was impressed there one night, however. He was at the bar with a mate, talking, but mainly perving on this gorgeous little number in a tight vest, white satin shorts and cowboy boots who was boogieing around in front of Jee at the door. A fair lump of a bloke at the bar, near Les, in a white suit and white shirt done up at the collar, finished his drink, looked at his watch, then walked over to the girl, put her over his shoulder and tossed her into the back seat of a Rolls-Royce convertible parked outside; and they both drove off laughing like drains. Les declared to his mate that if Charles Bukowski was still alive, even he'd call that style. The thing that impressed Norton most about Redwoods though, besides the food and the people, was that it was just down and around the corner from his house and he could fall out the front door blind drunk and be home in bed in less than ten minutes. Then stagger back for a good breakfast the next day.

'So that's where I mainly go for a drink on my nights off, Garrick. I don't know if that's true about the owner. But if he's there you can ask him. He sounds like he might be in your line of business.'

The major looked thoughtful. 'What did you say his name was again?'

'Marty. That's all I know.'

'Mmhh. Oh well. The place sounds interesting.'

'What do you like to drink?'

'Just Jim Beam and soda. Slice and ice.' The major smiled. 'What about you, Les? Darwin Stubbies?'

Norton smiled back as they walked along. 'You wouldn't believe it, Garrick, but since I got back from Hawaii, I got a taste for that Millers Genuine Draught. In the long neck.'

'Seppo beer!?' retorted The Gecko. 'Shit! What are you, Les? A bloody poofter or something?'

'Yeah,' nodded Norton. 'And they got it freezing cold round there. I drink crates of it.'

The major shook his head. 'Oh well, to each his own, I suppose. You don't have a float in the Gay Mardi Gras, do you, Les?'

Norton shook his head also. 'Not since the horse died.'

They wheeled right at the bottom of Hall Street into Campbell Parade. There were more people around now; walking, licking ice-creams, sitting in restaurants

107

or whatever. At Redwoods, the door was open and Jee was standing at the front in a pair of jeans and a brown silk shirt. His big friendly smile seemed to get bigger when he saw Norton.

'Les, my man, how's it goin', brother?'

'Pretty good, Jee. Okay if me and my friend come in for a couple of cool ones?'

Jee made a magnanimous gesture with his hands. 'Please do.'

Norton tossed the major a wink. 'What did I tell you? You don't get a much better welcome than that.'

'You're not wrong,' agreed The Gecko, following Les inside.

'Hey! Look at that,' said Les. 'There's two empty seats at the bar.'

The place was reasonably crowded and before the major knew what was going on, Les had threaded them through the tables and the people and they were propped on two stools on either side of the corner; The Gecko on Norton's right at the short end; Les at the start of the long end of the bar. The barman knew Norton of old, gave him a smile and, before long, Les had an MGD in his hand and the major had his Jim Beam: slice and ice.

'Well, cheers, Garrick,' said Norton. 'It's nice meeting you. Certainly different, but nice all the same.'

The Gecko clinked Norton's bottle. 'I think I'd have to say pretty much the same about you, Les.'

Norton's first beer went down pretty easily, so he ordered another. He remembered the major said he was more a moderate drinker so Les just left some money on the bar and told Garrick that if he wanted anything, get it and take it out of that. The major nodded a thanks and seemed quite happy just to sip his bourbon and look at the people around him. Les took another swallow of beer and did pretty much the same.

There appeared to be the usual laid-back crowd having an early Wednesday night drink or a bite to eat. All the seats at the bar were taken, there were a few tables of girls on their own, or boys and couples picking at their beef carpaccio, chargrilled tuna or whatever. Les didn't notice anybody he knew, or the owner, or any singers, actors or young billionaires; just happy, casually dressed people enjoying themselves while a bit of M. People wafted from the speakers round the walls.

The only exception appeared to be five drunken men in working gear, dirty jeans, King Gee shorts, boots and whatever, swarming around the end of the bar near the coffee machine. One was wearing a BLF T-shirt and Les tipped them to be off the building site next door. They'd probably been working overtime, decided to have a couple of beers at Redwoods because it was handy, got the taste and stayed ever since. Now they'd reached the good old obnoxious-Australian-yobbo stage. Les had worked and played football with a lot of building workers. Most of them were okay and out to make a dollar the same as everybody else. But a lot of blokes Norton came across in the building game had the attitude that they were the only people in the world that did any work. And anybody that didn't pour concrete or whatever and drive round in a Holden ute with a concrete-mixer and a blue heeler in the back and drink fifty schooners in the public bar with 'the boys' after work was a bludger and a soft cock.

The five men at the other end of the bar appeared to have that attitude. Especially a tall one with brown hair and an overgrown moustache plastered across a snarly, fat pie-shaped face. Les ordered another two drinks and he and the major sat there absently watching as the five yobbos gave the 'bludgers and soft cocks' around them a bit of aggro; trying to hit on the girls, making lots of noise, spilling their drinks, etc, while they engaged in a bit of push and shove and gave each other a few friendly head butts. Good yobbo stuff. The patrons around them tried to ignore them as best they could. Jee came over a couple of times and politely asked them to settle down; they mostly ignored him then gigged him and gave him the finger behind his back when he walked back to the door. On the third trip back, Norton noticed Jee's usual sparkling smile was starting to fade and tipped they might get a bit of action in Redwoods before the evening was over.

'Who are your mates down the end of the bar?' the major said to Les.

Norton shook his head. 'I dunno. They're probably off that building site next door.'

'Do you think they'd have a brain between them?'

Norton shook his head again. 'If they did, it'd be in mint bloody condition.'

After two beers on top of all that food, Norton thought he might switch to bourbons also. He was about to order another round when he noticed The Gecko watching something at the end of the bar. 'Pieface', the tall builder with the moustache, tired of annoying everybody else around, had decided to start on the staff and, with his yobbo mates egging him on, was in an argument with the barman. Despite the music and the surrounding noise you could hear the builder bellowing at the top of his voice and it appeared to be over a dollar or so. The barman, a skinny kid with a black ponytail and a stud, who was probably a part-time model, was trying patiently and politely to explain to Pieface that if you ordered bourbon, you got house bourbon. If you wanted Jim Beam, Wild Turkey or whatever, it was extra; in this case it came to a dollar. But Pieface would have no part of it. He'd definitely been robbed and he had it all over the young barman who was just trying to do his job, so like a big man he was going for it. Making plenty of noise and making a complete flip of himself in the process. The other barman was helping the manager do something, so the barman with the ponytail was on his own. Les was trying to catch his eye when a blonde in a tight blue top, sitting on The Gecko's right, waved some money in the air. The barman, looking for an excuse to get away from Pieface, saw her, excused himself from the builder, and came up to take her order. Pieface would have no part of that either. As soon as the barman made it to the blonde, he elbowed his way through the patrons, charged round the corner of the bar and elbowed his way in between the major and the blonde to give the barman another gobful. With his face all red and his chest puffed up with belligerent confidence, Pieface jabbed his finger over the bar.

'*You will not walk away from me,*' he bellowed, trying to sound semi-intelligent and extra-tough by emphasising each word. 'You will be told. You won't tell me.'

'Yes, all right,' said the barman. 'Now, if you'll just

excuse me for a moment, I'll just see what this lady wants.'

Pieface looked like he was going to explode. 'Hey, don't you try and ignore me. I work for my fuckin' money, more than you do. And I know the price of drinks.' Pieface jabbed his finger at the barman, waving his arm around and, in the process, knocked some of The Gecko's drink over his hand.

The Gecko looked at his hand for a second, then turned to Pieface, turned to Les, then back to Pieface. 'Excuse me,' he said, tapping the builder on the shoulder. 'What seems to be your problem, son?'

Pieface turned and glared down at the major. 'No one's fuckin' talking to you.'

'I know they're not. But they're spilling drinks on me, and I don't very much like it.'

'Well, I don't give a fuck what you like. Mind your own fuckin' business.'

Jee seemed to sense something was going on from where he was standing at the door. But he was too preoccupied with another bunch trying to get in to come over. Les also got a sense that it might be a good time to slip his watch off.

'You appear to be concerned over a dollar,' said the major, ignoring Pieface's last statement. 'Well, there's five,' he said, taking some money from the bar and offering it to the builder. 'Why don't you take that, settle down, and join your friends back at the end.'

'Why don't you take your five dollars and shove it up your arse,' snarled Pieface. He jabbed a thumb in his own chest. 'And I'll fight anybody.'

'Yes, you probably would,' said The Gecko, putting

the five dollars back with the other money. 'No doubt you're one hard man.'

Very casually, The Gecko rose from his stool and, in about the same movement, slammed his left knee in the builder's groin. Pieface's eyes stuck out like two button-squashes as the pain and shock hit him. Just as quickly, The Gecko banged the palm of his left hand up under the builder's chin; nothing very fancy, but it almost broke his neck. His head barely had time to snap back, when the major grabbed him by the front of his jeans, brought him forward and at the same time smashed the top of his skull into the builder's face. His nose crumpled, blood bubbled down into his moustache and that was the end of him. The major twisted Pieface around, kicked his legs away with a foot sweep and the builder crashed onto a table, then the floor, out like a light. Which, apart from the screams of a few girls and the startled looks of the nearby patrons, should have been the end of it.

But no. Pieface's mates came running up from the end of the bar, the same time as Jee came running in from the front door. The leading yobbo grabbed the stool Major Lewis had been sitting on and, dying for a sneak chance to belt the black doorman all night, he swung it into Jee's face, stopping him dead. Jee went down on one knee and the yobbo crashed the stool across his neck. Going well, the yobbo went to bring the stool down on The Gecko's head. The major moved in slightly, blocked the stool with his left hand and drove his fingers up under the yobbo's floating rib like a knife. The builder just had time to screw his eyes up and give a gasp of pain, when The Gecko brought his

113

right arm up and hammer-fisted the yobbo across the bridge of his nose, smashing it like Pieface's, then kneed him in the back as he went down. The stool hit the floor, and the other patrons leapt up, heading for the exit signs, figuring there was quite a problem arising now, and tripping over Jee and Pieface in the process.

This left three drunken yobbos still keen for a bit of aggro. The first one, a big, heavy-set dill wearing the BLF T-shirt, jumped on The Gecko's back and they both crashed to the floor. It all happened pretty quickly and Les was happy sitting there, watching the major in action. Now he decided he'd better do something; at least break the fight up, if nothing else. Les would have, only just as he rose from his seat, he spotted the yobbo to his right go to king-hit him. Les tucked his chin in and brought his shoulder up and the big left haymaker bounced off the top of Norton's thick, red Queensland skull. Oh well, thought Norton, looks like I'm in this now, whether I want to be or not. He bent at the knee and slammed three quick left hooks into the yobbo's face. The first two mangled his lips to pulp and knocked out several teeth, the third one just sent a spray of blood all over the wall and the nearest Aztec mural. That was enough. But Les decided to finish him with a short right that swung his jaw round to the other side of his face. He hit the deck cold just as the last yobbo threw a flurry of lefts and rights at Norton. A couple landed, but Les blocked most of them with his left and drove a straight right into the yobbo's face, squashing his nose all over it. He shut his eyes just as Les bent at the knee again and threw a sizzling left uppercut that caught him right on the point of the chin, almost driving his jaw up into his skull. He headed for the deck, also, and just before he did Les grabbed him by the scruff of the neck and banged his head against the bar, putting a split in his scalp about a foot long. With them out of the road, Les turned to see how the major was doing.

The Gecko was on his back with the huge builder over the top of him pinning him down; there was very little movement. Les was about to kick the yobbo in the head when The Gecko spun round from underneath the builder and finished up on top of him. He had both sides of the yobbo's T-shirt collar in his powerful hands and had ripped them across his throat, effectively choking him out. It was nothing fancy again, just close-quarters combat, but the yob's eyes had glazed over, his breathing had stopped and he was about five seconds away from dying. Instead of kicking the yobbo in the head, Les tapped The Gecko on the shoulder.

'Excuse me, Major, but is he really worth killing? And we wouldn't want to jeopardise the mission now, would we?'

The Gecko's head swivelled round to Norton and he looked up with that smiling, unsmiling lizard look on his face. 'Yes, you're right, Les,' he agreed. 'Good lad.' Major Lewis let go of the yob's throat. He sucked in a horrible, rattling gasp of air as his head hit the floor and he went to sleep.

Jee was on his feet now, a little battered and a little bruised, but not bleeding, so Les thought it might be as good a time as any to get out of the place. The bar staff and the manager saw what happened. They could clean the mess up and Norton was definitely a much preferred customer to the five dummies snoring and bleeding on the floor.

'Are you okay, Jee?' Les asked the big American.

'Yeah, I think so.' Jee blinked his eyes, moved his neck and looked at the yobbos lying amongst the upturned chairs and tables on the floor. 'Shit! What happened here?'

Norton patted him on the shoulder. 'If anybody asks, Jee, *you* did it.' Les nodded to the door. 'There's a dump-bin in front of that building site. Throw them in there till they sober up.' He turned to The Gecko. 'Come on, Major. We'd better get going, I think.'

The major nodded. 'Good idea, lad. Good idea.'

They threaded their way through what startled patrons were left and headed for the door. As he got to the footpath, Norton realised he'd left a fairly hefty tip on the bar. Oh well, he shrugged, it was only Price's money anyway. He and The Gecko got into double time along Campbell Parade, swung a hard left back into Hall Street and were crossing Consett Avenue almost level with the Post Office when the major spoke.

'I thought you said that was a quiet bar, Les? With good clientele.'

'Normally it is,' replied Norton. 'I don't know how those mugs got in there.'

The Gecko shook his head. 'The way that big bloke was going on. Terrorising that poor kid behind the bar. *And I'll fight anybody.*'

'Yeah, he was going all right, until you kneed him in the nuts.'

The major made a gesture with his hands. 'Normally I don't do those sorts of things. It's just that he was big and I felt threatened.'

'You felt threatened?' Les tried not to burst out laughing. The Gecko had just taken out three big men in about a minute and he 'felt threatened'.

'Yes, Les. Threatened and frightened.'

'Well, dear me, Major. Don't you ever feel threatened. I mean, not when you've got me around. Shit! That's what I'm here for — aren't I?'

'Yes,' nodded The Gecko. 'I was watching you from on the floor. You don't throw a bad left hook — for a young bloke.' The Gecko nodded again. 'Yes, you're right, Les. I never really thought of that.'

Norton was still trying not to laugh, and also trying to figure out whether The Gecko was laughing or not, when they'd crossed Six Ways and were back inside the flat. They both had a bit of blood on them, so Les suggested that if the major wanted to use the bathroom, Les would use Susie's en suite and they could get changed out of their smoky, dirty clothes. Garrick thought this was a splendid idea and about ten minutes later, they were both in clean T-shirts and jocks, standing in the lounge room.

'Well, what would you like to do now, Garrick?' asked Norton. 'Watch TV? There's a beer in the fridge.'

The major shook his head at the offer of a beer and looked at his watch. 'I wouldn't mind doing a few more calculations and a bit of mucking around for another hour. Then how about we watch "Star Trek". Do you like "Star Trek", Les?'

Norton smiled and made an expansive gesture with his hands. 'Hey, Garrick. You're talking to a fair dinkum trekkie here.'

'Yeah?'

'Reckon,' nodded Les. 'It's my favourite show. Who do you like best? Data? Or that counsellor with the big tits?'

'Ohh, no contest,' said The Gecko. 'Give me Counsellor Troi and those grouse tits of hers anytime.'

Major Lewis went into the bedroom and closed the door. Les got a beer from the fridge and fiddled around finishing another tape. A little over an hour later they were on the lounge watching their favourite TV show. It wasn't a bad episode either. A mob of shifty Romulans had tried to sneak in under the Star Ship Enterprise's guard and cause havoc. But Captain Picard, Lieutenant Worf and the team kicked their Romulan khybers all the way to the other side of the galaxy. Plus Counsellor Troi got changed out of her uniform and they had a bit of a perv on her boobs. They watched the start of 'Letterman'. But ten minutes later both men were yawning. The major had been up early and Les had had a big one the night before. He switched the TV off and they hit the sack. Minutes later Norton was staring at the universe and thinking once again that Major Lewis still didn't cease to amaze. What next, Norton wondered. Oh well. Before long, Les had beamed himself well and truly out and was soaring and snoring peacefully into the cosmos.

Around eight the next morning, Les was seated in the kitchen, finishing breakfast. He'd got up earlier, walked down and bought the papers in Hall Street. Now he was flicking idly through the *Telegraph Mirror* while he sipped his coffee. Les didn't have the radio on and there wasn't a great deal in the papers and what there was didn't interest him all that much. What Norton was mainly thinking about was his new flatmate, Major Lewis. When he said The Gecko never ceased to amaze, he sure wasn't kidding. The way he took those three dills out at Redwoods was beautiful to watch. Even if it was only plain, simple unarmed combat. Then he didn't even talk about it afterwards. Les knew heaps of blokes, they get into a bit of a scuffle, and what was just a few punches thrown turns into a knock down, drag 'em out brawl lasting half an hour. Then they go on like heroes and never shut up about it. The Gecko half killed his three blokes, then went home and watched 'Star Trek'. He had style. For some reason, despite only knowing him a short time, Norton found himself liking Major Lewis. The Gecko was definitely a man after his own heart. No matter what he is, mused Les as he sipped his coffee, he sure never ceases to amaze. I wonder what next? Les heard the bedroom door open, there were noises in the bathroom and a few minutes later the major was standing in the kitchen wearing a faded pair of blue tracksuit pants and an equally faded Newcastle Knights T-shirt.

'G'day, Garrick,' said Les, brightly. 'How's it goin'? You sleep all right?'

'Yes, I did thank you, Les. That bed's quite comfortable. How about you?'

'Like a top. I had a bit of a big one the night before. You fancy a cup of coffee?'

'Yes, I wouldn't mind. That smells good.'

'The plunger's over near the sink. If it ain't warm enough, just pour a cup and stick it in the microwave.'

The Gecko smiled and rubbed his hands together. 'Okey doke.'

Les flicked through the *Tele* some more while the major fossicked around in the kitchen. Before long, he was seated in front of Les with a coffee and a toasted cheese and tomato sandwich. Les offered him the *Herald*. The major declined, saying he might read the papers later on. Les continued to read. There was no conversation, The Gecko just sat there eating his toasted cheese sandwich, silently watching Les. By the time The Gecko had finished his cheese sandwich, he'd managed to completely psych Les out. Les put his coffee down and closed the paper.

'So what were you thinking of doing today, Major?' he said.

The major eased back in his chair, folded his arms

and looked directly at Les. 'I wouldn't mind getting a bit of exercise.'

'Suits me,' replied Les. 'It's not a bad day outside. Bit cloudy. But it's hot enough. What do you want to do? Have a run or something?'

'I was thinking more of a walk.'

Norton nodded, understandingly. 'Fair enough.'

'Do you know any good, long sets of steps around here, Les?'

Norton had to think for a minute. 'Yeah. Down at Tamarama Gully. There's a set of steps run from there up to Birrell Street.'

'Okay. We'll go there.' The major stood up. 'You be ready in ten minutes?'

'Yeah,' nodded Les. 'But give me time to clean up first. The landlady's a bit of a fusspot.'

'Yes. I've noticed that,' replied the major. He rinsed his cup and plate in the sink. 'And I think that's a good thing to see.'

Fifteen minutes later, they were out the front. The major had his Brooks on, plus a sweatband and dark sunglasses. Norton looked much the same. Shorts, an old T-shirt, Nikes, sunnies and a sweatband. They did a few stretches against the letterboxes, where the major was easily as flexible as Les. Les didn't see Macabee or anyone else much around while they loosened up. They did a few more deep breaths and squats and things. Les glanced at his watch. The major gave the word. Les said to head towards the baths. He'd show the way after that. And they walked off, down Hall Street, then cutting into Lamrock Avenue.

The major didn't quite walk, he marched, swinging

his arms in short arcs across his waist like a Russian marine; and he took long strides. Norton was expecting maybe a brisk stroll. This was more like a forced march, almost a jog, as the major moved briskly along like a small express train. Finally Les fell into step, and before long they'd crossed Campbell Parade, passed the baths and were marching solidly along the path around the little bay in the cliffs known as The Boot because of the big rock sitting there that looks like one. They passed that and came to the set of sandstone steps that ran up from the bay.

The major stopped at the bottom and looked at Les. 'These aren't the steps you were talking about, are they?' he said.

Norton shook his head. 'No, we've got about a kilometre to go yet.'

'Oh, good then. Okay, after you, Les.'

Norton trotted up the steps with the major one step behind him. They followed the cliff path to the next set of steps that led up to Mackenzies Point, climbed those easily, marched down to Mackenzies Bay, past Tamarama Surf Club, then crossed Pacific Avenue into Tamarama Park. Norton was puffing a little and he had a good sweat up when they stopped where the concrete path ended, under the trees, alongside the old sandstone wall and where the steps zig-zagged at first, then wound up to the corner of Cross and Birrell Streets.

'How do they look, Major?' he asked.

The major looked up at the long, steep set of steps, glanced around at the surrounding houses and flats above Tamarama Gully, and smiled at Les. 'These will do just fine, Les. An excellent choice, lad.'

'Good.'

The major smiled at Les again. 'You ready then?'

Les nodded.

'Well, come on. Let's go.'

The major certainly didn't take the steps like a cute little gecko lizard. He went up them in a crawling sort of sprint like a big goanna. It was uncanny and, besides that, Les didn't think anyone could move so fast. Les was taking the steps two and three at a time just to keep up with him. How long it took to reach the top, Norton didn't know. He was too busy sucking air into his lungs and hoping his leg muscles wouldn't burst when they did. The major's chest was heaving when Les arrived next to him. But his breathing was steady, his face was lit up and he was still full of beans.

'Well, that was good, Les. I enjoyed that.'

'I'm glad you did,' puffed Les. 'My ring's hanging out. You sure took me by surprise.'

The Gecko smiled. 'Come on, let's go down and see if we can do it again.'

'Sure. Why not,' said Les.

'But going back, we do it my way, Les.'

Norton was looking forward to the trot down the stairs. It would be a chance to get his breath back, now he knew more or less what to expect. Except the major went down backwards. Les tried to get in step and it was horrible. It was as if someone was dragging him backwards, down some crazy ladder that went everywhere. Les bounced off the walls, the rails, and fell on his arse twice before he caught up with the major waiting at the bottom of the steps. Les had time to arrive, take a gulp of air and figure out which muscles were going which way when The Gecko smiled and pointed back up the steps.

'Are you right for another one, lad?'

'Sure,' heaved Norton. 'Why not. After all, I'm here to look after you, aren't I?'

'I know, Les,' smiled The Gecko. 'I think that's probably why I feel so good.'

Ten times The Gecko took Les up the steps and back. By giving it everything he had, Les was able to reach the top, four or five steps behind him. But coming down was a mess. Norton thought he had the gist of it a couple of times before he'd either go on his arse or almost break an ankle. When he'd reach the bottom, he'd find the major waiting with his breath back, ready to go again. The major didn't actually race Les, or deliberately try to humiliate him. He just casually and cunningly managed to make him look like a big wally. Les came blundering backwards down the stairs for the last time, gasped in some air and rested his hands on his knees.

'Well, that's ten times, Major,' he panted. 'How many more you want to do? I'll admit it, mate. I'm rooted.'

'No. That was a good workout,' conceded The Gecko. He was puffing almost as much as Les and it was obvious he'd had a good hit-out too. 'We both went well.'

'I'm half a chance of going up with you,' said Les. 'But coming down, you make me look like I *should* be pushing a float in the Mardi Gras.'

The Gecko smiled. 'You should try it more often, Les. It's good for your co-ordination.' The major

124

stretched his arms out. 'Come on, lad. Let's head back to the flat. Apart from all the bloody dog shit everywhere, I rather enjoyed that walk around the cliffs.'

Les fell into step with the major and sweated along. He was able to keep up all right, except his leg muscles were all over the place. That backwards down the stairs threw him right out. Just goes to show, mused Les as they marched past Tamarama Surf Club, you think you know everything. And you know bloody nothing. Yes, sir, Major. You sure do never cease to amaze.

Back at the flat, it wasn't quite a race, but they both dived into the fridge pretty smartly and drank all the cold water Susie had in the filtered container. Les refilled it and suggested once again to the major that if he wanted to use the bathroom he would get cleaned up in the en suite. The major agreed and got out of his sweat-soaked T-shirt. After having a shower, Les changed into a pair of Levi shorts and a white Banana Republic T-shirt he'd bought in Hawaii and was staring into the mirror. What he was mostly looking at was his aching, throbbing legs; mainly his thigh muscles. All he kept relating to was Wiley Coyote in 'The Bugs Bunny Show', when he swallows a whole jar of 'leg muscle pills' and his thighs swell up like a mini-dinosaur. That was how Les felt. The major's idea of a walk was something Norton wouldn't forget in a while. Walking or jogging backwards was tricky enough at the best of times, but sprinting backwards down the Birrell Street steps was something else again. Then just like Wiley Coyote, when the light bulb switches on over his head and he gets some sort of crazy idea, Norton's eyes narrowed and he got that same stupid half-smile on his face also. He'd go back to those steps and get it all together. Then he'd invite Billy Dunne for a quiet jog and see how he went. The light bulb went out over Norton's head and he walked slowly out to the kitchen to find the major in a pair of shorts and a white singlet, with a glass of water in his hand, flicking through the *Herald*. He looked up as Norton entered.

'I might go out and have a read on the sundeck for a while,' he said.

'Okay, Garrick,' answered Les. 'I'll do a bit more taping. You want to have a bit of lunch later on?'

'Yeah,' nodded the major, 'that sounds good.'

There was a kind of old lounge chair on the second sundeck and a small table. The Gecko took both papers and his glass of water out there, sat down and started reading. Les poured himself another glass of water too, then went into the lounge room and began flicking through Susie's CDs again. He put five in the stacker, placed the headphones on and gingerly sat down on one of the padded footstools. Les was starting to feel good after the workout; except that every time he bent his knees, he thought his thigh muscles were going to burst and spray ligaments, sinew and blood vessels all over the walls.

None the less, Norton was enjoying himself, tapping his feet and nodding his head to the music, as he finished the tape from the day before and started on another one. He'd taped plenty of tracks that caught his fancy: 'Evening Sun' by Ronnie Earl and The Broadcasters, 'Baby, Please Don't Lie To Me' by Mike Morgan and The Crawl and was tossing up whether to tape an unfamiliar version of an old soul number, 'Hold On, I'm Coming' by Solomon Bourke, when he felt a tap on his shoulder. Les took the headphones off and looked up. The Gecko was either smiling down at him or he wasn't; Norton couldn't tell which.

'Les, give me about four or five minutes, then come out onto the sundeck.'

After all the non-stop rock 'n' roll through the headphones, Les wasn't quite sure what he said. 'Sorry, Major. What was that again?'

'Give me about five minutes,' repeated The Gecko, 'then come out onto the sundeck.'

'Yeah, righto,' replied Les absently, as the major turned and went back out to where he'd been sitting.

Norton glanced at his watch, looked at the CD cover he was holding and decided to tape Solomon Bourke while he pondered what the major was on about. Maybe he'd found some sheila sunbaking in the nude on another sundeck or something. Norton got the track down, removed the headphones and walked out onto the sundeck. The Gecko was seated facing Hall Street. Norton leaned back against the balcony and looked over at him.

'So what's — ?'

'Les!' The Gecko beamed up. 'How are you?'

Norton gave him a bit of a double blink. 'I'm good. Yeah, terrific.'

'Come over here, Les. Squat down on my right, as if I'm about to read you something out of the newspaper.'

'Yeah, righto,' shrugged Norton. He walked over and squatted a little painfully down next to the major.

The major ran his finger across the page, then turned

and smiled at Norton. 'Les, did you know this block of flats was under surveillance?'

'What!?'

'Don't start looking around,' said the major quietly, turning back to his newspaper. 'Just look at where I'm pointing in the paper. Laugh. Pat me on the back. Then go back to where you were standing.'

'Sure,' replied Norton, just as quietly. He waited a moment or two, tossed back his head and laughed, then did exactly as the major said.

Susie's second sundeck wasn't very big so, although the major was looking into the newspaper as he spoke, he didn't have to talk very loud to make himself heard.

'Behind you on your right, Les, there's a block of units. Glass rails on the balconies. Double white roller-door out the front. The window on the end, second flat up on the left. Turn around, look up and down the street a bit, then tell me if you can spot anything. Say something to me first.'

'All right.' Les pointed at the major and laughed again. 'That thing in the paper,' he adlibbed, 'cracked me right up.'

Norton shook his head, turned around and rested his hands on the balcony. He stared into the garden, looked down Hall Street, watched a couple of cars go past, then let his eyes drift over the surrounding blocks of units and houses and the flat the major had mentioned. Next to the sundeck, a white curtain flickered behind a sliding glass door. In the left corner you could just make out a slight reflection and a narrow, dark shape. Les gobbed into the garden, scratched his balls casually then turned back around.

'There's something in the front window,' he said.

'Mmmhh,' answered the major, turning the page without looking up. 'Someone up there has got a telephoto lens trained on this block of units. I think it's ASIO.'

'ASIO!!?'

'Keep your voice down, Les. Yes, I've got a feeling. I also think I saw your two Russian fishermen, too. A big, florid sort of bloke, and a younger, leaner one, wearing grey tracksuits.'

'Yeah, that's them.'

The major turned another page. 'They left about forty minutes ago. That old bloke was sitting out the front. He said something nasty to them in Russian then went back inside.' The major looked up at Les and sort of smiled. 'What was it you thought he said to them again, Les?'

Norton shrugged. 'He called them Chechibi or Caechibi bastards or something.'

'You don't think he might have been calling them KGB bastards, do you, Les?'

'Shit!' Les gave the major another double blink. 'I never really thought of that.'

'Mmmhh.' The Gecko went back to his paper and turned another page. 'There's something a little fishy, besides those two Russians, going on here, Les. In the meantime, why don't you jokingly pat me on the shoulder again as you walk past. And go back in the lounge and continue with your taping. I'll keep an eye on things out here for a while then we might go and have a bite to eat somewhere.'

'Yeah, righto,' said Les, sounding more than a little

mystified. He gave it a moment or two, then did exactly as he was told and went back in the lounge room.

Well, isn't that a nice turn-up for the books, thought Les as he continued with his taping. According to him, ASIO's watching the place. And I suppose he ought to know. I don't know about those other two being in the KGB. I think that's making the cup of tea a bit too strong. But if he's right about the other, what the hell are they doing watching this block of flats for? Surely it's not Susie and all her CDs. She's not smuggling microfilm or CD-Roms or something? Maybe that was her contact at the airport. I only got a glimpse, but he looked middle-eastern. Side Valve, a spy? Les shook his head. Hardly. A bit shifty maybe, but that's about all. Maybe it's Ackerley? The mysterious disappearing boarder, with his Star Trek posters and his books about the fourth dimension. He's a mad scientist. A time traveller. That cheap wardrobe in his room is really the Tardis and that's where he's hiding. Despite the levity, Les suddenly felt a little uneasy for a moment. What if ASIO are watching the major? No. Les shook his head again. If they were, he'd have told me. Or on the other hand he wouldn't have said anything at all. For a few more moments the gravity of what Les and The Gecko were up to flashed through Norton's mind. There was a chance things could go wrong. Very bloody wrong.

Les found another track he liked and taped it. 'Down Home' by Marty Stuart. While it was playing he tried, if not to see the funny side of things, at least the cynical side. Who did I say the major thought he was? Frederick Forsyth? No, it's John Le Carré. First we've got ASIO and the KGB. Next'll be the CIA and MI5. How about the Mafia? No, a Columbian drug cartel. What about the Russian Mafia? That's what those two fishermen are. Russian Mafia dons. They look more like Laurel and bloody Hardy. Boris and Igor. Les smiled thinly. That's what I'll nickname them. I'll call the big bloke Boris and the young one Igor. They're a couple of good Russian names, aren't they? Les finished the Marty Stuart track and still wasn't sure whether to start laughing or crying when he felt another tap on his shoulder. Les saw it was the major again and went to take the headphones off.

'You hungry?'

'What was that again, Garrick?'

'You feel like something to eat, Les?'

'Yeah, sure.' Norton switched the stereo off and stood up. 'What do you feel like?'

'Just a bit of schnitzel and salad or something. But not down the beachfront. A pub lunch amongst the punters'll do.'

'I know just the place,' said Les.

Norton suggested the No Names at the old Bondi Rex. The food was good, you could blend in with the crowd and it was only about ten minutes' lazy walk from the flat; or a three-minute forced march if you wanted to do it Gecko-style. The major put on a light blue cotton hang-out shirt and they headed out the door towards Glenayr Avenue, then Beach Road.

'So did you see anything else out the front, Garrick?' asked Les.

The major shook his head slowly. 'No, nothing much. A couple of blokes who came out of that block

131

of flats looked a bit suss. But . . .' The major shook his head again. 'No, nothing much.'

The major seemed to be thinking about something on the way down, so Les left him to it. If he wanted to tell Les anything he probably would. Les was trying not to think about the whole thing, but couldn't help it. All he kept saying to himself was 'Shit! I hope nothing goes wrong'.

One thing was for sure, there was nothing wrong with the food. There weren't many people left when they walked in the glass doors of the No Names, Bondi. They found a table between the kitchen and the back wall and had a chicken schnitzel and salad each, plus Les had a spaghetti and got two bottles of mineral water. The Gecko got into his schnitzel, had a taste of Norton's spaghetti and ordered one also; which he couldn't finish, so Les finished it for him.

'Well, how was that, Garrick?' asked Les, swallowing the last of his mineral water.

'Very good, Les,' replied the major. 'You've done it again. In fact, I wouldn't mind coming back here for another one of those chicken schnitzels.'

'Any time you want, Major Lewis, sir. I'm here to look after you.'

The Gecko smiled. 'I know that, Les. In the meantime, I'd like to do a bit of snorkelling this afternoon.'

'Snorkelling — as in skindiving?'

'Yes, but no wetsuits and weights and shit.'

'You want me to come with you?'

The Gecko shook his head. 'No, I'll go alone. Besides, after all that spaghetti, you're likely to sink.'

'Yeah,' laughed Les, 'you could be right.' Good, that

means I don't have to go home to get my gear and look at Warren and his moll.

'I just want to have a bit of a look round the front of the baths. Check out a couple of things.'

'You got enough gear?'

The Gecko nodded. 'Yes, I brought it all with me.'

'All right. When did you want to go? Now?'

'Why not,' agreed the major. 'By the time we walk back to the flat, then down the beach, the meal will have gone down admirably.'

Les paid the bill and they walked back to Susie's unit almost in silence; with the major again doing what appeared to be some heavy thinking. Inside the unit, the major said he wanted to make a couple of phone calls. Les said to go for it. He'd fix all that up with Susie when she got back from Melbourne. The major rang what sounded like his wife first, then somebody else. Les fiddled around in the bedroom while the major was on the phone, putting a few things in an overnight bag for the beach; towel, zinc cream, book, etc. Bad luck, no banana chair. Les slipped into a pair of thongs, then waited for the major in the kitchen. Not long after, The Gecko had his cap on, his overnight bag packed and over his shoulder, and a pair of thongs on also. Les punched in the security buttons and they wheeled out the main entrance. Who should be sitting out the front in his usual position, wearing his usual gear, but Macabee. Norton knew he should have kept his mouth shut. But the bloke was such a lemon he couldn't help himself.

'G'day, mate,' he said, with false good humour. 'Not goin' fishin' with your two friends today?'

Macabee spat on the footpath again. 'KGB bastards.'

'You're not wrong,' agreed Norton. 'They're all dropkicks.'

They got a few paces past the units when The Gecko turned to Les. 'I thought that was what the old bloke said.'

'Yeah,' agreed Norton again, only this time a little apprehensively. 'You could be right.'

They crossed Six Ways, went down Hall Street as far as the St Vincents at Jacques Avenue and then turned right and down to Lamrock Avenue. Les was content to let the major lead the way. They didn't talk much. Les mentioned a little about Hawaii and how he happened to be in Susie's flat. The major seemed to be listening, but he seemed to be thinking as much as he was listening, so Norton let it go at that. They crossed Campbell Parade and walked down the park, stopping in front of the railing at the end of the promenade while the major checked things out. A southerly was blowing with a few clouds around, so even though there were plenty of people on the beach, it was nowhere near packed. The tide seemed to be coming in with not much of a surf up but quite a strong rip running in the south corner from the rocks all the way to the baths; the baths looked to be deserted.

Garrick suggested they go over near the rocks in front of the steps before the stormwater drain, a little away from everyone, so Les followed him down the ramp and across the sand. Despite the breeze and the clouds there were still sufficient tits and bums to perv on as they trudged across the sand; and plenty of

134

blokes' ones too, if you were that way inclined. The Gecko chose a spot near a couple of rocks and Les scooped some sand out, placed his towel over one of the rocks, then sat down making himself as comfortable as possible without his faithful banana chair. The Gecko dropped his bag on the sand, too, and was soon down to his Speedos and a pair of ear-plugs. He wasn't super muscly, but had a wiry, hard frame with very little fat. Les also noticed he had pretty much the same snorkelling gear Les used in Florida; mini-fins, silicone mask and leak-proof snorkel and webs.

The major pointed to his watch. 'I should be back in an hour, but wait two hours. If something happens and I'm not back by then, ring Eddie. Okay?'

'Yeah, righto,' replied Les, a little concerned. 'Hey, everything's all right, isn't it? You want me to follow you round the rocks?'

'No, it's all right, Les. I'll see you in an hour.'

'Okay, then.'

The major walked down to the water's edge, stood inconspicuously amongst the other bathers for a few moments, then got into his diving gear and, keeping away from the surfers and boogie-board riders, drifted out in the rip running alongside the rocks. Les watched him floating out easily, till he got to the flat rock ledge where the baths start and began diving. It wasn't long before Norton lost him in the chop and the backwash coming from the ledge next to the baths. Oh well, thought Les, not much to do now. He shifted his backside into the sand, got his book from the overnight bag and began reading more Paul Mann. Every now and again he'd gaze out towards the baths in case he might spot the major. But no. So it was back to the book. And, in a way, Les couldn't think of a better way to spend an hour than sitting on the beach with a good novel.

It didn't take long for an hour of more murder and corruption in India to pass and Les started looking at his watch. An hour and ten minutes went by, then twenty minutes. After an hour and a half, Les put his book back in the bag and was concentrating on the ocean where the rip ran alongside the rocks and the baths. There was no sign of the major. Les had taken off his sunglasses and was standing on a rock looking out to sea, when he heard a voice behind him.

'I enjoyed that, Les.'

'What . . .?' Les got down from the rock and looked at the major who appeared to be covered in tiny goose bumps.

'I would have come in earlier, but there was a bit of a wave on one of the sandbanks. So I had a surf with my snorkelling gear on, then had a quick shower up near the railing. It was fun.'

'Fair enough. It's just that after ninety minutes . . .'

The Gecko definitely smiled. 'Good to see you're alert, Les. It's very gratifying to know I'm involved with someone I can trust.'

'Thanks, Garrick. But I am here to keep an eye on you, you know. If anything should happen, Eddie and Price'll kick my arse.'

'Sure,' smiled the major, getting his towel from his bag. 'Now, what say we start heading back to the flat. After an hour and a half out there, my quoit feels like it's frozen shut.'

'Okay,' said Les, putting his towel in his bag. 'I'll make a big pot of hot coffee when we get there.'

'Good idea, Les. You do make a mean cup of coffee.'

'Thanks, Garrick.'

The major dried off and got changed, put his diving gear back in his bag, and they walked over to the ramp, then over to the steps and back across the park towards Campbell Parade.

'So, what did you see out there, major?' enquired Les. 'Anything worth . . .?'

'No, not really,' answered the major. 'I was just checking out the rocks along the foreshore and different things. That wall facing the ocean is in worse shape than I thought. But nothing to get overexcited about.'

'That's good.'

They walked a bit further, when the major turned to Norton. 'Les, there's something I'd like to ask you.'

'Sure,' answered Norton, 'what is it?'

'If you were going fishing. You'd definitely use bait, wouldn't you, Les?'

Norton had to think for a moment. 'Well, that's the main idea of fishing, ain't it? A hook, on the end of a line, with bait on it, to catch fish?'

'Exactly what I thought, Les. So if you were going fishing. You'd use more than just a couple of big sinkers on the end of your line, wouldn't you?'

'Well, of bloody course you would.' Norton looked at The Gecko. 'What is this, Major, sir? Some kind of riddle?'

The Gecko started to laugh. 'No, Les, not a riddle. I was just asking you something, that's all.' The Gecko continued to chuckle as if he was laughing at some private joke. 'You know those two Russian fishermen? The ones I saw Macabee swearing at earlier.'

'Yeah,' nodded Les, as they approached Campbell Parade.

'Well, in case we see them around again, I've thought of a couple of good nicknames we can give them.'

'You have?'

'Yeah. We'll call the big one Boris, and the other one Igor.'

Norton gave The Gecko a double, triple blink. 'What was that again, Major?'

'We'll call the big one Boris. And his skinny mate Igor. They're a couple of good old Russian names.'

Norton stared at the smiling Gecko and nodded dumbly. 'Yeah. Yeah, you're right.'

'That's exactly what I thought, Les.'

Norton didn't know what to think as they crossed Campbell Parade and headed up Lamrock. What did I say earlier? Frederick Forsyth. John Le Carré. Now I'm in the bloody Twilight Zone. Surely the bastard can't read minds. Norton shook his head. This is starting to get a bit weird.

Not a great deal was said during the walk up Lamrock Avenue. Les was too busy thinking and, it seemed, so was The Gecko. Back at the flat, the major got under the shower and Les got another plunger of coffee together. Les was waiting for the electric kettle to boil and kind of pondering what the major meant about going fishing without bait and also still wondering whether he had some sort of strange ESP, along with everything else that was different about him, when the phone rang. The kettle had an automatic cut-out; Les left it, went to the lounge and picked up the receiver.

'Hello.'

'Hello, Les. It's Susie.'

'Susie! Hey, how are you, mate? How's things down there in Melbourne?'

'Terrific. Overcast, raining, cold — ideal weather for a funeral.'

'Yeah, well, that's Melbourne, Susie, ain't it?'

'Yeah. So how's things up there? Everything okay? You haven't wrecked my flat yet?'

'We had a bit of a party last night and someone threw up over your CDs and piddled on your lounge, but apart from that — it's been pretty quiet.'

'Thanks, Les. You know, sometimes I don't know whether to believe you or not.'

'No, it's all right,' chuckled Les. 'All I've been doing is sitting around taping your CDs and drinking all your coffee. I even met Macabee and those two Russian blokes.'

'That New Guinea Blue coffee's nice, isn't it?'

'Yeah, tops. Better than that lime tea.'

'So, everything's okay, Les? No phone calls?'

Norton shook his head. 'No, no phone calls. I haven't seen hide nor hair of your boarder either.'

'He'll get in touch sooner or later, I suppose. Listen, Les, what I'm mainly ringing you for is —'

'You're horny and you want me to come down,' cut in Les. 'Okay, I'll be on the next plane.'

'No, not that. Christ, Les! That's all you ever think of.'

'I can't help it, Susie. I'm sorry. You just bring out the animal in me.'

'Listen, seriously, Les. I forgot to tell you to pick up my mail. I'm expecting a couple of cheques.'

'Okay. Hang on and I'll go and have a look now if you like.'

'No, that's all right. Just leave them on my dressing-room table.'

'Okey doke, or, no worries, as they say in Melbourne.'

They nattered on for another minute or so about nothing much in particular before Susie said goodbye and that she'd probably see Les on Sunday. She didn't know what flight she was on yet. Les said to let him know and he'd pick her up at the airport. Norton put the phone down just as the major came out of the shower with a towel round him. Les looked up.

'That was Susie, the girl who owns the place.'

'She doesn't know I'm here, does she?'

Les shook his head. 'No. She just reminded me to pick up her mail, that's all.'

'Oh.'

The major went into his bedroom and shut the door. Les went into the kitchen and filled the plunger with boiling water. While it was brewing, Les thought he might as well go out and check Susie's letterbox for her. He left the flat unlocked, but took the keys to the main door.

There were three letters for Susie. An electricity bill, another one from Telecom, and what looked like a bank statement. Definitely no cheques though. Les had another look to make sure, when who should loom into

140

view coming up Hall Street, but the two Russians. Same grey tracksuits, same overnight bags, only the big man, Boris, was carrying the one fishing rod. Les caught the big man's eye and was almost about to say, 'Hello, Boris' when the bigger man spoke.

'Hello, my friend,' he said jovially. 'How are you today?'

'Pretty good thanks, mate,' replied Les. 'How's the fishin' goin'?'

'The fishing. Hah! Not so good the fishing.' Then the older Russian's face broke into a leathery, jowly grin and he made an expansive gesture with his hands. 'But you should have seen the vun that got avay.'

'Yeah,' replied Les, with a wink and a smile. 'That's the old story, ain't it, mate.'

The big Russian walked off hah-hahing and hoh-hohing at his own joke with the younger man following behind. Oh well, thought Les, KGB or not, the old bloke doesn't mind a laugh now and again. Yeah, he's got a really vild and vacky, vunderful sense of humour. Boris opened the front door and Les glanced up from Susie's letters just in time to see the younger man staring at him. Unlike the older man, it was an expressionless look and completely lacking in humour. If anything, it bordered almost on rancour. Don't know about you though, Igor, thought Norton. I think if you ever laughed you'd probably shit yourself. The door closed behind them and they were gone. Les closed Susie's letterbox and strolled back into the kitchen. The major was standing there, showered and shaved, wearing his tracksuit pants and a plain blue T-shirt.

'I think you've done it again, Les,' he smiled. 'That coffee smells sensational.'

'Yeah, I think it'll be okay,' said Les. He put the plunger on the table next to the cups and got the tin of Carnation Milk from the fridge. 'I just saw the two Russians out the front. Boris and Igor.'

'You did?' said the major, sitting down.

'Yeah.' Les sat down too. 'I think they just come back from the beach. Boris was carrying his fishing rod.'

An odd smile slipped across The Gecko's face. 'What did they have to say?'

Norton shrugged. 'I asked Boris how the fishing went. And he said, "You should have seen the vun that got avay." '

Major Lewis started to laugh; though it seemed to be at something other than Norton taking off the big Russian's accent. ' "The vun that got avay," eh. Boris has certainly got a sense of humour.'

'Yeah. That's vot I thought.' Les poured two cups of coffee. 'It's funny, though, his mate Igor gave me a real dirty look as they went in the door.'

'Did he now?' The major's smile seemed to disappear. 'That's interesting. That *is* interesting.'

They added the milk and sugar and began sipping away, enjoying their choice coffee. After being in the water so long, then getting cleaned up, the major especially seemed to be enjoying his. Les felt a bit of a wimp in a way, because the whole time they were on the beach he didn't even get his feet wet, let alone go for a swim.

'Well, Les,' said the major. 'It won't be all that long now and I'll be out of your hair.'

'You haven't been in my hair, Garrick,' replied Norton. 'I'm used to this sort of thing, hanging around with Price and Eddie. It sort of comes with the territory. No, to be honest, I've learnt a couple of things actually. And I imagine I'll learn some more tomorrow night.'

The major smiled and sipped his coffee. 'Les, if at times I seem a bit moody or secretive, don't let it bother you. It's just that I've had some things on my mind.'

'That's all right, Garrick. Shit! I imagine you would have.'

'Eddie sent me up some photos. But that old handball court's turned out to be a bit trickier than I thought.'

Les looked evenly at the major from across his coffee. 'In what way?'

'Well, it's all solid concrete underneath, but the building around it's a bloody mess. If I don't use enough explosive, I won't shift the substructure. Too much and I'm likely to bring the whole bloody lot down — including that caretaker's flat and whoever's in it.'

'Shit!' exclaimed Les. 'That'll be nice.'

'Yeah, but I think it's all sweet. In fact, that Ackerley left his word processor in his room, which has come in very handy. I've been mucking around on that, and it's all looking okay.'

'That's good.'

'The other thing, Les. I probably sounded a bit facetious when we were walking back from the beach and I was going on about fishing without bait or whatever.'

'Yeah, I was wondering about that,' said Les.

'Well, when I went diving this afternoon, I wanted to check out the baths. But I also had a feeling those two Russians might be down there, so I wanted to have a sneak look at them also.'

'Go on.'

'They're up to something, Les. I watched them head down the beach earlier. And a minute or so later, two young blokes from the block of units opposite followed them.'

'ASIO?'

'ASIO. CIA. FBI. All those college kids stick out like dogs' knackers. They're tailing them for some reason. Boris was dangling a line near the baths all right. But when I dived down, he had no hook on his line. He was just down there killing time.'

'He could have been doing the same thing when I saw him down there yesterday,' agreed Les.

'I couldn't see his mate Igor. But I'm sure I glimpsed him lurking around down near the baths yesterday. Did your friend Susie say something about them just moving in here?'

'Yeah, some old couple moved out for a while. And they moved in.'

The major gave Norton a mirthless smile. 'That's how they do it, Les. They find a couple of Russians living here. Make them an offer, and if they don't like it, threaten to shoot all their family back in Russia.'

Norton looked at the major for a moment. 'What do you think they're up to?'

'I don't know. That old bloke reckons they're KGB. They could be the Russian Mafia. But, at a guess, I'd say they're expecting a drug shipment.'

'Fair dinkum?'

The major nodded. 'That, or they're here to assassinate someone. Someone who probably goes fishing off those rocks near the baths. That's how they've picked up the two spooks.'

'Nothing to do with us?'

The Gecko shook his head adamantly. 'No. They're here doing their own thing, and by an unlucky coincidence, so are we.' A devilish little smile flickered across the major's face. 'They'll get a nice surprise on Saturday, when they go fishing and the back of the baths are gone.'

Les had to smile also. 'Yeah, I imagine they will.'

The Gecko eased back in his seat. 'So, that's why you might think I had the shits with you or something, Les. It's just that I came here to do one job, which could be a bit trickier than I thought, and I find this other rattle going on. Let's just say, it's given me food for thought, Les.'

'That's quite okay, Garrick.' Les was adamant too. 'I realise what's going on. And you just go right ahead and do what you have to do. Don't worry about me in the least.' Les smiled and give the major a wink. 'It's fun having you around, mate.' Which was true. Les *did* like Major Lewis. And now his openness and honesty about what was going on, and his consideration of Norton's feelings, made Les warm up to him even more.

'Well, that's good, Les,' smiled the major. 'If you behave yourself, I might even take you up those stairs again tomorrow — twenty times.' The major chuckled slightly at the dumbfounded look on Norton's face and poured himself another cup of coffee. 'So tell us a bit more about your trip to Hawaii, Les. What happened to that bloke you live with again? He got blown up in a volcano?'

Norton laughed and poured himself another cup of coffee also. 'He almost bloody did.'

They chatted away about different things that had happened to them in life. Garrick told Les a few stories of what he and Eddie got up to in Vietnam. Les told the major a bit about America and the time he and Eddie buried the painter and docker under the airport. The conversation was good with quite a few laughs thrown in and, despite daylight saving, it was soon dark and they both had coffee coming out their ears.

'I'm not a real big eater, Les,' said the major. 'But you know what I feel like now? A nice bowl of soup.'

'How about some matzo ball soup back over at the Hakoah Club?' suggested Norton.

'Perfect,' said The Gecko.

'You want to go now?'

'Okay, why not.'

Five minutes later they were out the front and about fifteen minutes after that, Les had signed his guest in and they were seated with their food in one of the booths that run adjacent to the back of the salad bar. Les decided he might just have soup too, plus some salads, bread rolls and mineral water. They didn't talk a great deal while they ate. Garrick seemed to like checking out the other punters and so did Les. It was the usual crowd — battling or well-to-do Jewish people, some with their children, enjoying the food, enjoying the company and talking their heads off while they

146

did. Les was attacking his bowl of Waldorf salad when he noticed The Gecko intently watching two solid men walking past their table. Les only made out their backs, but the major turned around and when he turned back he seemed to think for a moment before he started eating again. When they finished their meal and the mineral waters, Les had a quick glance at his watch.

'Well, how was that, Major, sir? Has your batman done it again?'

'Private Norton. You would be welcome in my company any day.'

'Why thank you, Major.' Les snapped the major his idea of a salute and got a zingy, crisp professional one in return. 'So what would you like to do now, Garrick?'

'Go back to the flat for a while, while I sort a few things out. Then I wouldn't mind having another drink at Redwoods. I imagine it would be all right.'

'Why wouldn't it?' said Les. 'We're the heroes of the day.'

They got up to leave and, as Les was tucking the back of his T-shirt in, he noticed The Gecko turn again and look behind them for a few moments. Next thing, they were back at the flat and the major went straight into his room. Les figured he had enough tapes done for the moment, so he switched on the TV. He probably wouldn't get any taping done tomorrow, but he'd catch up on Saturday and Sunday before Susie got back — if he wasn't blown to pieces or in gaol by then. Les was halfway through a re-run of 'NYPD Blue', when The Gecko came out of his room holding the *Telegraph Mirror* with a big, happy smile on his face.

He stood near the TV and looked down at Norton sitting on the lounge.

'Les,' he said slowly, 'you like your music, don't you?'

'Hang on.' Les hit the mute button on the remote. 'What was that again, Garrick?'

'You like your music, Les.'

Norton shrugged. 'Sure I do. Not that baby-boomer shit they play on the radio stations, but tracks I've never heard. Susie's got some great stuff there. That's the reason I've been going for it. Why?'

'You know, Les, I'm a bit miffed.' The major gave Les his little-Gecko-lost look. 'All the time I've been here, and you've never asked me once what sort of music I like.'

'Shit! You're right. I haven't. Sorry, Major. It's just that I was all wrapped up in what I was doing — I never thought . . . Okay, so what sort of music do you like, Major?'

'Guess?'

Norton had to think for a moment. Vietnam Veteran. *Tour Of Duty. Apocalypse Now.* 'The Doors'?

'The Beatles.'

'The Beatles?'

'Yeah, I got every one of their albums and CDs. They remind me of different times in my life. What about you, Les? Do you like The Beatles?'

'Me?' Les slipped into an off-key burst of 'I . . . should've known better with a girl like you. That I would love everything that you do. Oooh I need your love babe. Guess you know it's true. The long and winding road. Shit, Major! would you like another quick medley?'

'So you like The Beatles, Les?'

'Yeah, I got a few of their CDs. The early ones mainly. Plus *Sergeant Pepper's*.'

'Well, look at this, Les.' The major showed Les the *Telegraph Mirror* where he had it opened at the Entertainment Guide. 'Appearing tonight at the Cock 'n' Bull in Bondi Junction — The Beatnix. I saw them on 'The Money And The Gun' doing 'Stairway To Heaven'. And they're sensaish.'

'Yeah, I've seen them down The Woolloomooloo Hotel a couple of times. They're not bad.'

The major was almost pleading with Norton. 'Les, you've *got* to take me up there. Come on, you're supposed to be looking after me, and I've been watching the money Price gave you — there's enough left there for the cab fare and a few drinks. Come on, Les. Willya, willya? G'wan. Please, please.'

Norton thought for a moment and tried hard not to smile. 'All right, Major. Rather than have you put a choker hold on me and wreck my good Banana Republic T-shirt, I'll take you.'

The Gecko slapped Les lightly on the leg with the paper. 'I'll see you back out here in half an hour.' He returned to his room and closed the door.

Well, how about that, Les chuckled to himself. The galloping major's got Beatlemania. Will I take him up there? Hah! I'd look pretty funny trying to keep those headphones on with a broken neck.

Les watched TV for a while longer, then, leaving the TV on, he had a shave in Susie's en suite and changed into a pair of jeans and a maroon striped, button-down-collar shirt. When he came back out, the major was standing in front of the TV also wearing jeans plus a grey-check button-down-collar shirt. With his brown hair swept loosely across his forehead, he looked good and he was all smiles.

'So how do we get there?' he asked.

'Walk down to Six Ways and get a cab,' answered Les.

'Well, come on, Ringo. Let's go.'

'Okay. Joost give me time to fix noombers, John.'

Les tapped in the security code and they strolled out the front for the short walk down to Six Ways. Five minutes later they were in a taxi and about ten minutes after that they got out at the lights on the corner of Bronte Road and Ebley Street in Bondi Junction. The major was rubbing his hands together and Norton could hear the band finishing some song as they crossed Bronte Road. Les pushed open the glass doors out front of the hotel, paid the owner waiting on the till near the end of the bar, then after getting stamped by the bouncer, they stepped inside just as The Beatnix kicked into 'Honey Don't'. The band was up on stage at the opposite end of the bar, done up in their grey suits with no lapels, going for it and sounding more like The Beatles than The Beatles. The drummer, who was belting out the words as well as the beat, sounded exactly like Ringo Starr; the same Liverpool accent, the same nasally, monotone voice. Norton glanced at the major and it looked like his eyes were starting to glaze over.

'Les,' he grinned, gesturing with his arms, 'what can I say? They're sensational.'

Norton smiled back. 'Do you want a drink?'

'Jim Beam and soda. Plenty of ice. Thanks, mate.'

Les left the major near a table beneath the bank of TV sets above that end of the bar and went over and placed his order with the dark-haired barmaid. While he was waiting he had a bit of a look around. It was quite a reasonable crowd for a Thursday night, mostly wearing T-shirts and jeans or dressed very casually. There were quite a few girls standing around on their own, jigging along to the music. Some of them were good sorts, but most were pretty plain and definitely none of them were starving. Les returned with the drinks to find the major doing a bit of Chubby Checker to 'Twist And Shout'. Norton gave him his drink and joined in a little with the major and the other punters boogieing around him. The major threw his Jim Beam down fairly smartly, so Les went to the bar for another two and came back just as The Beatnix slipped into 'Eight Days A week'. It was a good singalong — the band had the punters going and, with a couple of Bourbons under his belt, Norton was glad now they'd came up. The Beatnix finished that song then slipped into 'Can't Buy Me Love'.

'I might go down a bit closer,' said The Gecko.

'Okay,' replied Les. 'I'll wait up here under the TV sets.'

With his drink in one hand, the major twisted and shouted his way through the crowd, disappearing somewhere near the speakers. Yeah, go for it, Garrick, Les smiled to himself, happy just to stand up the back and listen to all the old Beatles songs and happy that he'd managed to show the major a good time again. Les had a few more drinks while the band played what seemed like an endless variety of songs before some of the lights came back on and they took a break, saying they'd be back soon with the second half of the show. Les got another bourbon and waited back under the bank of TV screens for the major.

Almost fifteen minutes went by and he didn't return, so, feeling a little concerned, Les decided to go and look for him. He couldn't see him in the crowd and he wasn't near the speakers. Then Les spotted him between the end of the bar and the pinball machine against the wall and a slight shudder went through Norton's body. The major wasn't in a fight or an argument or trying to kill anybody. It was worse. He was chatting up two girls — a blonde and a brunette — and doing pretty good; he was cracking jokes and the girls were laughing. The blonde was hanging off his arm and didn't look too bad. But her girlfriend should have been out biting a postman or in a backyard somewhere, digging up someone else's old bones. And they were both pissed.

The major's girl was around thirty, tall and gangly with no tits, frizzy blonde hair and an acne-scarred face heavily covered with make-up. Two clumps of red plastic hung from her ears and she'd squeezed her skinny behind into a pair of white jeans, matching white boots, a red T-shirt and a white jacket. Her girlfriend wasn't as tall but she was four times as heavy with dark hair, spiky on top and long at the sides over a long, dark face and long, dark lips. Despite another thick coating of make-up, a visible moustache covered her top lip. There was a mole on her chin and her eyebrows met in the middle. Her outfit was a pair of baggy black jeans with white stitching, a black T-shirt and a blue collarless top with four big, white buttons down the front. Standing in the flickering light of the pinball machine, she somehow reminded Les of a Klingon. The major caught Norton's eye and happily gestured with his drink.

'Les. There you are. Come over and meet the girls.' Norton walked over and the major introduced the blonde first. 'Les, this is Doreen, and this is Coral.'

Norton did his best to smile and make eye contact. 'Hello, girls,' he said, 'nice to meet you.'

'Hi, Les,' they seemed to chorus.

'Doreen was just saying to me,' said the major, 'she said, "Frank, you're one of the nicest blokes I ever met." Didn't you, Doreen?'

The blonde nodded enthusiastically and smiled at Norton. 'I did, too. He's lovely,' she said, and cuddled up closer to The Gecko.

Norton understood. 'Well, that's nice, Frank,' he said. 'I'm real glad for you.'

The major smiled his Gecko smile at Les, pleased that Norton had picked up his message. Then, before Les could get a chance to put his foot in things, he started tap-dancing away with some conversational spiel, managing to give Les a quick briefing of the situation at the same time. Both girls worked as typists for the same oil company at Botany and both lived in the same flat at Coogee. They originally came from Lithgow and had been living in Sydney for two years. 'Frank' had told them he was the Town Clerk at Ballina, down for a conference, and he was going back tomorrow. When the ball landed in Norton's court, Frank returned it for him, saying Les was a truckdriver for Ballina Council. He said that Les was his driver and that he was going back to Ballina the next day also. They were both staying at Les's sister's place in Bondi. Whatever it was The Gecko told them, it went over as smooth as custard, as they slurped happily away on the second round of Bacardis the major had bought them. Doreen was all over The Gecko like a cheap suit and, with Norton trying to be nice just for the major's sake, Coral was giving Norton a few very heavy once-up-and-downs as she started inching up a bit closer to him.

Les downed his bourbon and unleaded, and rattled the ice in his empty glass. 'I'm going to get another drink. Anybody else want one? Girls?'

The major shook his head. 'No need to,' he said, 'the girls are going.'

'Oh?' said Les, trying hard not to show his joy. 'That's a bit of a shame.'

'Yeah, but it's all sweet, Les. We're going with them.'

Norton's joy evaporated even quicker than it began. 'We are?'

'Yes,' cooed Doreen, snuggling up closer to The Gecko. 'Me 'n' Coral were going to go because we were hungry. And Frank said he'd take us out for dinner and drinks. Isn't that lovely?'

'Dinner? Drinks?' said Les. 'Where?'

'What was the name of that place you said we were going to again, Frank?' said Coral.

'Redwoods,' smiled The Gecko. 'Down at Bondi.'

'And we're going to have sushi,' said the blonde,

smiling at Les as she held onto the major. 'I've never tried it, but it sounds really nice.'

'Neither have I,' said Coral. 'But I'll give it a lash. I'm starving. What about you, Les?'

Les nodded blankly at her. 'Yeah,' he answered, just as blankly. 'I suppose I could eat something.'

'Well, come on then,' said The Gecko. 'Let's go.'

Norton's eyes were starting to bulge a little. He stared at the major and desperately pointed to where the band was getting changed behind the speakers into the Sergeant Pepper's uniforms for the next bracket. 'What about . . .?'

The Gecko made an offhanded gesture. 'We'll catch them next time we're in town. Right now, I've got to catch some fish for sweet little Doreen here's sushi.'

'Ooh! Isn't he lovely,' squealed the blonde.

Les nodded flatly. 'Yeah, one of the best,' he muttered.

Before Norton could do or say anything else, the others finished their drinks and they were out the front of the hotel where a taxi happened to be waiting at the lights. They bundled in; Les in the front, the major and the two lovelies in the back. The taxi headed towards Bondi Beach with the major pissing in the girls' pockets and cracking more jokes in the back, while Les fumed silently in the front. Isn't this lovely? he growled to himself. You can bet your life he'll want to drag the two of them back to Susie's place so he can try and get into the blonde's pants. And in the meantime, I've got to walk into Redwoods with that wobbegong on my arm. Oh God! Norton shook his head. Still, you never know. It might be a quiet night and there'll be no one in there I know. Or maybe with a bit of luck we're both barred because of that fight and they won't let us in. Anything, please. The Gecko prattled on in the back about absolutely nothing, while Les tried to bury himself in the front seat. They cruised down Bondi Road before stopping for the lights at The Royal Hotel. As they drove off, Les suddenly felt a soft typist's hand come over and lightly stroke his neck; it gave him both goose bumps and sent a shudder running down his spine. When the taxi stopped outside Redwoods, the driver gave Les a lurid wink as if to say, 'You're on a good thing, mate'. They bundled out and Les paid the fare.

Despite Norton's hopes and prayers, his luck was right out and things couldn't have been worse. Jee was on the door and his big, happy face broke into about a hundred smiles as soon as he saw them. Jee shook Norton's hand and thanked him for helping to get rid of the five mugs the night before; Les had been right earlier when he jokingly told Garrick they'd be the heroes of the day. Jee greeted the major like he was a member of the royal family and treated Coral and Doreen as if they were Nicole Kidman and Madonna. Then, when they walked inside, there were people Les knew everywhere. Joe Heets, the bloke that put the girl in the back of the Rolls-Royce, was standing at the bar with two models. Another bloke Les knew who ran the surf shop just up the road was there with two of his waxhead mates and another bloke Les had met that owned a yacht; they were talking to a team of young glamours from the north-side surfing scene. Every table was packed with well-dressed men or women who were either eights or nines. And I'm standing here with Phyllis Diller and the Klingon, thought Les, as everybody in the place that knew him seemed to smile and nod hello at once. Oh well, at least there's no empty tables. That means we'll have to go out the back where no one can see us. But no. Norton's run of bad luck continued. No sooner had they walked in, when four people seated along the corner of the bar got up and left.

'Hey! How lucky's that,' said the major, and herded them towards the empty barstools.

Les sat on the end barstool next to the wall, underneath the glass cabinet containing the Redwoods T-shirts. Coral sat next to him, then the major and Doreen. Norton had just squeezed his backside onto the barstool when an arm snaked around Coral and an empty hand appeared next to him. Les pushed $200 into the empty hand, it disappeared and the major started playing Champagne Charlie. Margaritas? Of course, girls, crooned The Gecko, waving fifty dollar bills everywhere. They go down splendidly with sushi. The Margaritas soon arrived along with the food waitress and a bourbon for Les, while he tried to hide as best he could in the corner. Isn't it amazing what a good time you can have when you're spending someone else's money, he thought, watching the major give the barman a tip that would have fed a family in Somalia for about a year. Yes, I'm so glad I was able to show the major a good time again. Around him, everybody he knew was either staring at them or taking quick glances. You could bet word about the fight would have got round and they were whispering about that. You could also bet they were whispering about why Les was in there with his mate, spraying up two drunken scrubbers.

Another round of Margaritas and a bourbon for Les arrived on the bar about the same time as two large sushi platters, complete with bowls of soya sauce and little wooden chopsticks wrapped in paper. Sitting on the two wooden boards, it looked all very neat, very dainty and very tasty. Oh well, what the fuck thought Norton. He wasn't a mad sushi fan, but he may as well have a pick. He broke open a pair of chopsticks, stirred some horseradish into a bowl of soya sauce, dipped one into it and started chewing away along with a pick of pickled ginger. Although, to Les, sushi was an acquired taste, it didn't go down too bad. The major didn't bother with his chopsticks and Doreen and Coral didn't know what they were eating, so they weren't going to stuff around trying to shovel whatever it was into their mouths with two little, wooden knitting needles. If you could dunk donuts, you could dunk sushi. In minutes, there was rice, ginger, splashes of soya sauce and everything else, from one end of the wooden platters to the other and across the bar. Les was no epicurean, but he couldn't remember the last time he felt so embarrassed. He put his chopsticks down and sucked on his bourbon.

'Hey, this stuff's not bad!' squealed Doreen.

'Yeah. It's all right,' said Coral. 'I don't know about that green shit though.' She dug her elbow into Norton's ribs. 'What d' you reckon, Les?'

'Yeah, terrific,' grunted Norton. 'Makes you want to go and live in Japan.' Les sucked on his bourbon and wished he was somewhere else while the others wolfed into the raw fish. Then he noticed something. So far that night, the major only had eyes for Doreen; he'd been all over her like a cake of soap and it wasn't half obvious what the Town Clerk from Ballina was after. Doreen was more than likely thinking the same thing. Between dunks of sushi, The Gecko took a brief look round the bar and for a moment it was almost as if he'd seen a ghost. He turned back to Doreen, who was talking to him and, although he was listening and trying to smile, it was obvious he was taking absolutely no notice and his mind was somewhere else. They dunked some more sushi and slurped some more Margarita when Coral decided she wanted to go for a pee. And Doreen, being a good Australian girl, decided there was no way she was going to let her mate pee on her own. They both left, taking their handbags with them. Les thought this was as good a time as any to tell the major he was on his own — Les was beating a retreat. Laying down his arms. Surrendering. Call him a coward if you will, sir, but if he had to look at the mole on Coral's face anymore, and her moustache, he'd bring up the one piece of sushi he'd had, all over the mess they'd made on the bar. Les was about to say something when the major leaned across to him, his back turned slightly towards the bar. The Gecko smile wasn't there either. Some other look was.

'Les, listen to me for a minute,' he said quietly and possibly a little urgently. 'Did you say the bloke that owns this place is called Marty and he made his money flying helicopters during the Gulf War?'

'Yeah, something like that,' answered Les. 'Why?'

'You see those two blokes sitting at the bar, next to that big bloke in the white suit?'

Les looked over at Joe Heets, who was still chatting happily away to the two models. He was standing, and sitting this side of him were two stocky, fit-looking men around thirty in jeans, T-shirts and loose-fitting cotton jackets. One had dark hair, the other more ginger; both looked foreign in some way. They were laughing over their drinks, but Les noticed their eyes were as hard as ball-bearings and every now and again, one of them would look towards the front door.

'Yeah, what about them?' asked Les.

'They're two agents with Mossad.'

'They're what?'

'They're an assassination team with the Israeli Secret Service. I know them — Zin Moise and Leo Glazer. I saw Leo's brother in that club earlier this evening.'

Les remembered The Gecko looking around in the Hakoah Club earlier. But he half had the shits now, being lumbered with Coral, and he wasn't quite in the mood for anymore ASIO, KGB, MI5, Mossad or whatever bullshit. 'So? They're probably only in here having a drink. Same as everybody else.'

The Gecko drew his face almost up to Norton's. 'Les, have a look what's hanging off the bar in front of them.'

Norton glanced over again. Hanging from the bar by their handles were two spring-loaded, fold-up umbrellas. 'Okay, so they brought their brollies with them.'

'Les, what was the weather like outside tonight?'

Norton shrugged. 'Warm. Bit cloudy maybe. That's about all.'

'It definitely wasn't raining, was it?'

'No.'

'Les, they're not quite umbrellas. They're sub-machine guns with silencers. I've used them. They're in here to hit the owner. I know who he's been working for.'

'You do?'

'Yeah, the Syrians. Anyway, it's got nothing to do with us. And I don't give a stuff who they kill. But as soon as those two sheilas get back, we're out of here.'

Norton was still a bit sceptical and wondering if this wasn't some ploy just to get Doreen back to the flat for the giant porking. 'Garrick, you are fair dinkum? This isn't just . . .'

'Les, as soon as the sheilas get back, I'll find some excuse and we make tracks.'

'Why not leave them here and just get on the toe ourselves,' Les suggested.

The Gecko gave Norton a very heavy, close-quarters once-up-and-down. 'Les, what do you take me for? Some sort of a cad?'

Norton was about to say something when who should come bowling through the front door in a pair of Levis and a plain white shirt, casually smoking a cigarette, but Marty the owner.

He had a quick word with Jee, said hello to some people seated near the door, shook a couple of hands, then moved along the bar, stopping to have a word with Joe Heets, before going behind the bar and stopping again next to the till. If Les had any doubts about the two men the major pointed out being killers, he needn't have bothered. As soon as they spotted Marty, their faces turned to stone and you could almost see their antennae go up. In almost one movement, they pulled a forty-round magazine out from each of their jackets, grabbed their umbrellas off the bar, jammed the clips in and rose to their feet — just as Coral and Doreen came up the steps from the toilets. Marty's instincts as a combat helicopter pilot were still with him. Just as the two Israelis started blazing away, he jerked his tall, gangly frame to one side, shoving the barman to the floor as he did.

The silenced Mini-Uzis didn't make a great deal of noise, just this burping, rattling cough, along with the smoke and sparks coming from the barrel. However, there was plenty of other noise and confusion. The hail of bullets smashed all the liquor bottles on the shelves, tore through the wooden closet, smashed the blender to pieces, along with the bowl of fruit, scattered the paper money pinned to the shelves, ripped up the muppet doll and tore shards of wood, concrete and plaster from the walls. Bullets were ricocheting and whining all over the restaurant amidst the clatter from the empty casings hitting the wooden floor. How they never cut Marty in two or injured anybody else was a mystery. After shoving the barman to the floor, Marty was jumping and jerking around behind the bar like Ben Turpin in an old silent movie, while the bullets kept zipping and whining all around him. Women were screaming now and half the restaurant had made a beeline for the front door. Doreen and Coral were frozen up against the wall behind the two Mossad assassins with bullets smacking into the wall above them sprinkling their hair with dust, concrete and plaster. Marty made a dash for the exit at the end of the bar as the two Israelis opened up on him again.

'Shit!' cursed The Gecko. 'I'd better do something before somebody gets hurt.'

He grabbed one of the unopened sets of wooden chopsticks, ripped them apart and scampered down behind the bar in a kind of running crouch. He crept up behind the red-haired Israeli, rose slightly and jammed the thin, wooden chopstick straight into his ear canal. The Israeli howled with pain and made a grab for his ear with one hand while his other hand flew up and emptied the machine gun across the ceiling, gouging out lumps of plaster and chopping the rotating fan to pieces. The other Mossad killer turned round just in time for The Gecko to ram the other chopstick into his eye. He roared with the agony and shock, dropped his weapon and grabbed at his face. The major then turned and grabbed the bewildered Doreen and Coral and herded them towards the front door, leaving the two Israelis cursing and groaning as they tried to pull the chopsticks out of their heads. Norton thought this might be as good a time as any to make a move too; one ricocheting bullet had missed his head by about a foot and shattered the glass in the T-shirt cabinet. He got up from his stool and joined the others. Jee was standing inside the door, his eyes bulging out like ping-pong balls, wondering what to do, when Les and his team shoved past him along with the rest of the crowd surging out into, then scattering up, Campbell Parade.

'Jesus bloody Christ!' said Doreen. 'What the hell was that all about?'

'It seems somebody wasn't happy with their sushi,' suggested The Gecko, herding the two girls towards Hall Street.

'I told you up at the Cock 'n' Bull not to come here,' said Les. 'The place has always had a dud rap on the food.'

'I dunno,' said Coral, 'I thought it was nice.'

'Yeah, well you know how it is,' said Les, 'some people are very fussy when it comes to sushi.'

The Gecko showed great concern over Doreen, asking her if she was all right, and dusting flecks of plaster from her hair while he slipped his arm around her. She was too drunk and stupid to know any different when the major suggested that a nice, strong cup of coffee would be the thing now for her nerves. That was quite an experience she'd just been through for an unsuspecting young country girl. Doreen smiled, put her arm around the major and kissed him on the cheek as they headed up Hall Street towards Susie's flat, with a reluctant Les and an equally drunken and heavy-breathing Coral bringing up the rear. The major kept himself busy putting work on Doreen. Les wasn't in the slightest bit interested, so the conversation between him and Coral was limited to the excitement of life in the typists' pool at the oil company and the exciting life she led in Lithgow before moving to Sydney. She tried to get close to Les, but after running up and down those steps with the major earlier, it was easy to keep a couple of steps in front of her. It wasn't all that long before they were there. Les fumbled the keys from his

164

pocket, hit the buttons and the light switches and they were all standing in the lounge room. Doreen and Coral gave Susie's unit the once-over and the first thing they both said at once was, 'Shit! Look at all those bloody CDs.'

'Yeah,' said Norton quickly, 'but the CD player's stuffed. So if you want any music it'll have to be tapes or the radio.'

'Oh, what a bummer,' said Doreen, putting a B52's CD back with the others.

The major turned to Norton. 'Les, I hate to impose, but do you think you could rustle up another plunger of your fabulous coffee? You're much better at it than me.'

'Yeah, righto,' answered Les. At least while he was in the kitchen he could avoid the Klingon.

'Whereabouts is the loo?' asked Coral.

'In there,' pointed Les.

'I'll go when you're finished, Coral,' said Doreen, and settled down on the lounge next to the major.

'I might put on one of the tapes I made up, Frank,' suggested Les.

'Yeah, good idea, Les,' replied the major.

Les put a tape on, turned it down a little, and, with Larry Boone twanging his way through 'Hotel Coup de Ville', he went into the kitchen and put the kettle on. Norton had absolutely no intention of putting any work on Coral. If anything, he felt shitty having her back at Susie's unit in the first place. It was a situation Les would have preferred not to be in, but it was the major's call and there wasn't a great deal he could do. However, he'd be polite and not say anything for the major's sake. And here I am, mused Les, as he got the

165

cups and spoons and whatever together. The polite little maid again. He heard the toilet flush, then voices in the lounge room and the next thing Coral was standing behind him in the kitchen.

'Do you want a hand, Les?' she purred.

'No, it's quite all right thanks, Coral,' said Les. 'I've got it all together. The kettle's almost boiled, the coffee has to draw, and that's it.'

Coral edged a bit closer. 'I'd like to draw you, Les.'

'What with? Oils?' Les forced out some laughter at his own weak joke. 'I mean, you work for an oil company. It's a . . . I say it's a gag, boy.'

'Don't go on silly, Les. I meant I'd like to do a sketch of you. I have been to art class, you know.'

'Really. I've never met an artist before. We don't have many in Ballina.'

Coral moved closer again. 'You'd make a great subject, Les.'

'Depends what you want to subject me to,' said Les. 'Oh goodness, is that the kettle boiled already? Coral, would you take that stuff on the table out to the others while I get this together.'

Coral breathed back from Les, giving him a very heavy once-up-and-down. 'Okay,' she said.

Les didn't know what to think while he waited for the coffee to draw, so he didn't think about anything. Just punt high and follow through and hope for the best. He'd get out of this somehow, without stuffing things up for the major. But no matter what, he wasn't porking Coral. No bloody way. The major could bayonet him, blow him up, shove chopsticks down the eye of his dick — a man can only not do what a man can only not do. Or words to that effect. Les took the plunger of coffee and placed it on one of the coffee tables where Coral had put the tray containing the cups and things. Susie had two double lounges set against the wall. Garrick and Doreen were intertwined at the end of the one on the left. Coral was seated on the other. Oh well, thought Les. He poured coffee into all the cups, then sat down on Coral's right facing the stereo.

'Ahh, well done, Les,' said the major. 'Good on you, mate.' He released himself from Doreen and picked up a spoon. 'Wait till you taste this, Doreen. My driver brews the best coffee in Australia.'

The two girls stirred in their milk and sugar and took a sip.

'Ooh, yes. It's really lovely,' said Doreen.

'Mmhh, great,' breathed Coral.

'Well, I do my best to please,' said Norton, taking a sip himself.

They settled back, sipped their coffee and listened to the tape Les had playing. Nobody said if it was good; nobody said if it was bad. The conversation was again very limited. The Gecko was too busy blowing in Doreen's ear and she was giggling and tittering away like a little budgerigar, or a long, skinny one. Coral was eyeing Les over the top of her coffee cup, giving him her oily, sweet Klingon smile, biding her time.

'So how do you like working on the council up in Ballina?' she said. 'It looks like it keeps you fit.'

'It's a good, honest job,' intoned Les. 'And with the overtime, I get a good, honest wage.'

'I don't mean that,' said Coral. 'I'm not interested in your money — honey.'

'Yeah,' said Les. 'What are you interested in? My truck? It's a Volvo F86 Table Top with a bogie-drive tipper. Goes great since we modified the clutch.'

'You didn't say crutch. Did you, Les?' purred Coral.

'No!' Les was adamant.

'Oh, okay then. We'll just put it down to a slip of the tongue.' Coral ran her tongue over her top lip and all the hairs on her moustache glistened with a moist, slick sheen.

Norton shuddered and wished he'd kept his mouth shut and said nothing. There was a sudden movement to his right as the major and Doreen rose from the lounge hand in hand and, without consulting anybody, went into his bedroom and closed the door behind them. Norton chuckled to himself and glanced at his watch. I reckon in about five or ten minutes, you'll be able to hear the screams coming out of that room at Norah Head lighthouse. If it wasn't for Lieutenant Worf sitting next to me, I reckon this could turn out to be a funny night. Les caught Coral's eye for a second and a thought briefly flashed across his mind. A blow job? No, no not even that. Not with a new BMW and house on the Gold Coast thrown in.

'Well, that leaves just you and me, Les,' said Coral, inching closer.

'Yeah, it sure looks that way,' answered Les. 'I don't see anybody else around.'

Coral put her coffee down and moved right up next to Les. Norton tried to get away, but she had him pinned on the end of the lounge.

'Righto, Les,' she said. 'Let's stop fucking around. Come here.' Coral put her hand on Norton's leg and tilted her face up to kiss him.

Coral mightn't have been a Klingon, but it smelled like she'd been eating Klingon dog food. Her breath would have scorched white ants out of a rotten verandah. Norton took one whiff and jerked his head away. 'Aarrgh! Yuk!' he gagged.

Coral glared up at him and her dark face got darker. 'What's the matter?' she snapped.

'Nothing,' said Les. 'Nothing's the matter.'

'Something's the matter.' Coral drew back from Les. 'It's me. That's what it is. There's something wrong with me, isn't there. What is it?'

'No,' said Les. 'It's not you, Coral. There's nothing wrong with you. It's . . .'

'It's what!?' Coral was getting steamed up.

'It's . . . it's . . . it's me.'

'You!? What the fuck's wrong with you?'

'I . . . I'm gay.'

'You. A poofter?'

Les nodded happily. 'Yeah, that's right. A poof. A horse's hoof. Camp as a row of tents, Coral. Punched more donuts than the Red Cross during the Second World War.'

Coral glared at Les and slunk back against the lounge. 'Oh shit! A bloody poofter. I don't believe it.'

Les nodded and shrugged his shoulders. 'Yeah. That's the way it goes these days, Coral. You just can't tell any more. Rock Hudson. James Dean. Me.'

Coral threw her arms across her chest and exhaled sharply. 'I should have bloody known though. All those muscles. You're probably just an aerobics princess. You shit yourself when the trouble started in the bar. If it hadn't been for Frank, we'd have still been there.'

'I know,' confessed Les. 'It's awful. The main reason I'm down here is to deliver the parts for our float in the Gay Mardi Gras.' Les smiled and fluttered his eyes at Coral. 'Did you watch the Gay Mardi Gras last year, Coral?'

'No! I did not!'

Yeah, I didn't think you would, you homophobic bitch. 'All right. But will you promise me one thing, Coral. Truly, I mean it.'

'What!?'

'Please don't say anything to Frank. He's my uncle. He's also President of the RSL. And it would break his heart.'

'Yeah, all right,' grunted Coral.

'Oh, thanks, Coral. You're so sweet.'

Coral turned and gave Les a sardonic smile. 'Hey, Les,' she said. 'You know what GAY stands for, don't you?'

'No, what?'

'Got aids yet?'

'Hey, that's not bad,' beamed Norton 'You got any more?'

Coral gave Les a quick, hostile once-up-and-down and slunk further back on the lounge. Les gave an inward sigh of relief and folded his arms also. Well, this has turned out all right, he smiled to himself. I've got rid of Lieutenant Worf. And any minute now, the fun should start when the major starts shoving that ten-pound Danish salami of his up poor skinny Doreen. I reckon the first screams should bring down Ackerley's old Star Trek poster. Then the ones in the lounge room. Les settled back, listened to his tape, and waited.

Five, ten, almost fifteen minutes went by; not a sound from The Gecko's room. Nothing. Not even muffled voices. The light had gone out. But nothing. Les was confused. Coral was bored shitless. She reached over and turned the music up loud. Les didn't give a stuff. He was more interested in what was going on in Ackerley's room. Jesus! He must be a slow starter. Then an awful thought hit Les in the pit of his stomach. Christ! I hope she hasn't knocked him back and he's murdered her. Garrick can be a bit odd at times.

Another twenty minutes went by and Tom Petty and the Heartbreakers were belting out 'Making Some Noise', when there was a sharp, loud rap on the door. Coral didn't seem to take any notice. Wondering what was going on and, hoping it wasn't the police, Les got up and looked through the spy-hole. It appeared to be a woman. He opened the door.

She was about sixty with a dour, plump face and grey-blonde hair and was wearing a powder-blue brunch coat. She looked like either a John Laws listener or Alan Jones; maybe Ron Casey. More than likely all three. 'Yes,' said Norton politely. 'What can I do for you?'

The woman gave Norton a smile that needed scaffolding to stay on her face. 'I'm the chairperson of the Body Corporate. Would you mind keeping the music down. It is getting rather late, you know.'

'Yeah, sure,' apologised Les. 'I'm sorry. I didn't

realise it was so loud. I'll fix it right now. Sorry . . . miss.'

The chairperson of the Body Corporate's smile creaked up about half a centimetre. 'Thank you.'

The woman's unit was adjacent to Susie's; she closed her door about the same time Norton closed his. He turned the stereo down then sat on the lounge near Coral.

'What was that?' she grunted.

'Julian Clary. He wanted to know if I just raided the council dog pound.'

'What!?'

'Some woman wanting me to turn the music down.' Les then ignored Coral and went back to listening to the music.

Another twenty minutes or so went by and the tape began playing the reverse side. Coral was tapping her feet impatiently on the floor and Les was beginning to get a little concerned. He was thinking of either switching on the TV or knocking on the major's door to see if they hadn't fallen asleep or something when there was the sound of voices and the light came on under the major's door. A few moments later the door opened and they both came out. Doreen's hair was all over her head and her clothes were a bit wrinkled. The major had his tracksuit pants and a T-shirt on; his hair, too, was plastered all over his head, his face was red and streaked with sweat and he looked like he'd just run a triathlon. Doreen went straight to the bathroom, the major gave Les and Coral a brief, weak smile then went straight to the kitchen and poured himself two long glasses of cold water from the fridge. He gulped one down, drank half the other, then brought it out into the lounge at the same time Doreen came out of the bathroom.

With her bag over her shoulder, she looked down at Coral. 'You ready to go?'

'Reckon.' Coral got her bag from the lounge and stood up.

'We'll get you a taxi,' said the major.

'No. That's all right, Frank.' Doreen gave the major a quick peck on the lips. 'See you next time you're in town. Thanks for the meal.'

'It was . . . my pleasure, Doreen.'

Les batted his eyes at the Klingon. 'Nighty night, Coral. See you next time I'm in town, too.'

'Yeah.' Coral didn't bother to look at Les.

The major opened the door, then closed it and they were gone. Although the music was still playing and he'd hardly spoken to Coral and not seen all that much of Doreen, it seemed strangely quiet after they had left, like there was a kind of tension in the flat. Les heard the front door close and the two girls' footsteps down the side just as the major flopped down in one of the lounge chairs and gulped down some more water. Les was about to say something when the major spoke.

'I'm absolutely stuffed,' he said. He tilted his head back and closed his eyes, took a couple of deep breaths, then opened his eyes again and looked at Les. 'So anyway, what happened out here? Or am I being a trifle indiscreet?'

'What happened out here, Garrick?' replied Les. 'Nothing. Zilch. A big fat zero.'

'Nothing?' The major seemed surprised. 'I thought you were a walk-up start?'

'To be honest, Garrick, that sheila was a beast. I'm not Brad Pitt, but she looked like a Klingon. Plus her breath smelled like a pig that had been eating rotten turnips.'

The major tried to laugh, but he looked too exhausted. 'Not a bad comparison, Les. I thought with that mole on her chin, she looked more like one of The Borg. The only thing missing was the tubes coming out of her head.'

'Yeah, thanks, Garrick,' Les looked directly at the major. 'So what happened with you? Christ! You were in there long enough. Or am I being — a trifle indiscreet?'

'What happened with me?' The major slumped back further in his seat. 'Les, you're not going to believe this, but the skinny Doreen had the biggest fanny I've ever seen.'

Norton gave the major a massive double blink and slumped back in his seat also. 'She what!!?'

'It was a monster. I banged and bashed away, but I didn't even touch the bloody sides. That's why I took so long. At one stage there I thought I was going to have to shove that boogie-board of Ackerly's through my braces so I wouldn't fall in. Either that, or throw in a few shovels' full of blue metal to take up the slack. It was a horror show.'

'She had a big ted?' Les stared at The Gecko, scarcely believing what he was hearing.

'Big? I bit her on the snatch, Les, and my head went straight in up to my shoulders. And there was a bloke inside walking around with a horse and cart, trying to light a hurricane lamp. He yelled out to me, "Hey,

174

mate, have you got a match? Mine are wet." In the end I had to think about my wife so I could empty out.'

Norton shook his head slowly with disbelief. Again, he didn't know whether to laugh or cry. Again, the major never ceased to amaze. Suddenly Les felt tired. This whole scene with the major was just getting too weird.

'Anyway, Les,' yawned the major. 'I am absolutely knackered. I don't know whether sweet Doreen got rooted, but I sure did. I'm going to have a quick shower and go straight to bed.'

Norton nodded blankly. 'Not a bad idea, Garrick. I wouldn't mind putting my head down myself. Tomorrow's the big day.'

'Yes, it certainly is, Les.'

Les gathered up the cups and saucers and put them on the tray to take into the kitchen. 'I'll see you in the morning, Major.'

'Yeah, see you then.' The major stood up, rocking a little tiredly on his feet. 'Oh, and Les, thanks for taking us out tonight.'

'A pleasure, mate. See you in the morning.'

Les put the tray in the kitchen, then went to his bedroom about the same time the major limped into the bathroom; he'd stripped down to his jocks and was cleaning his teeth in Susie's en suite when he heard the shower running. He looked at himself in the mirror, shook his head, then turned off the light and crawled into bed. Well, that's another day over, he thought as he stared at Susie's star map on the wall. Norton's thoughts suddenly drifted from the star map back to the bullet ricocheting into the glass cabinet just above his head. And in a way, I'm lucky to bloody be alive again. Coral was half right about me shitting myself. When those two Mossad blokes opened up, I was too busy gawking around to duck down behind the bar. One thing for sure, I'll never ignore anything that major says again. If he says black is white, black *is* bloody white. Or vice versa. Les chuckled to himself. What about his girl Doreen though? Shit! If what he said was true about her ted, I wouldn't mind it full of antique dressing tables. And what about poor Coral? She thought she'd found herself a real man and all she got was a big poof that drives a Volvo. What if Billy and the boys find out? I can't wait to tell them. Les yawned and shoved his face further into the pillows. Anyway, tomorrow's the big day — or night. I hope it doesn't stuff up. After tonight though, I'm just about ready to give up. I couldn't give a stuff one way or the other. Les gave another yawn and, before long, he'd zoomed off into the galaxy once more and was snoring soundly.

Around nine the next morning, Les was sitting in the kitchen in his jocks and a T-shirt, sipping coffee, after eating an apple. He'd woken up earlier, sometime before seven, after hearing noises in the bathroom, then the sounds of someone cursing and doors slamming as they tried to start a car out the front. Les dozed off again and, with his sleep disturbed, slept in longer than he meant to. The major's door was slightly ajar and the kettle was still warm sitting near the kitchen sink, but there was no sign of the major. Les took another sip of coffee and stared impassively from the kitchen into the lounge room. An apple and a cup of coffee wasn't quite the ideal breakfast; but it was all Les felt like at that time. Today was 'nuke the handball court day' and, despite his previous sentiments, Les was hoping it all went smoothly. 'Nuke the handball court day.' Norton smiled mirthlessly over his coffee. The day of The Gecko. Or night. Take your bloody pick. Les was still staring into the lounge room when the front door opened and the major stepped quietly and easily into the kitchen, wearing his tracksuit pants and a white T-shirt and carrying the *Telegraph Mirror*.

'Hello, Les,' he said, dropping the paper on the table and opening the fridge. 'How are you this morning?'

'Pretty good, Major,' replied Norton. 'How about yourself? You sleep all right?'

'Like a top.' The major went to the sink and poured himself a glass of cold water. 'But six or so hours was plenty.'

'Yeah, I heard you get up earlier, but I thought, "bugger it", so I went back to sleep.'

'Fair enough.' The major put the container back in the fridge and sat down facing Les with his glass of water.

'So where have you been?' asked Les. 'Round the lovely Doreen's having breakfast and a morning glory?'

'No,' smiled The Gecko. 'I woke up a little after six, fart-arsed around doing something for a while, then went for a bit of a stroll.'

'Down the baths?'

The major shook his head. 'No, but I did go past your favourite drinking hole.'

'Was it open?'

The major nodded. 'And doing a roaring trade.' Garrick opened the paper to page five and pointed to a small paragraph at the bottom. 'Read that,' he said.

Les looked at where the major was pointing. All it said was, 'Patrons were startled when a man discharged a starting pistol at a Bondi restaurant late last night. There were no injuries. Police are still investigating.'

'Don't try and tell me your Jewish mates at your club down the road haven't got some tug round here. You saw what happened last night.'

'Saw what happened? A bloody bullet missed my head about two bloody inches.'

'Exactly. So Yom Kippur, Les.' The Gecko smiled and raised his glass of water.

'Yeah. Shalom,' replied Norton, half raising his cup of coffee.

The Gecko sipped his glass of water and looked directly at Les. Norton avoided his gaze. He wasn't all that keen to talk about the previous evening's events. Apart from the band, it was one of the lousiest nights Norton had ever spent. Les was half looking at something in the paper about Christopher Skase when The Gecko folded the paper back up and placed it at the edge of the table. Not that Les gave a stuff. It was the major's paper and he could do what he liked with it. He still kept staring at Les as if something was burning his arse. Les looked at him, then looked away again. Finally the major spoke.

'Les, what are you doing right now?'

Norton shrugged. 'Nothing much. Just sitting around like a stale bottle of piss. I might go for a run or something later, unless you've got something else planned for us.'

'Stay there for a minute, lad. I want to show you something.' The major went to his room, then came back with a book and several sheets of foolscap paper. He placed the sheets of paper on the kitchen table with the book on top, then sat down and resumed staring at Les. 'During the festivities in my room last night, when I was bedding the fair maiden, Doreen, this, along with just about everything else in the room, fell down on the floor.' The major handed the book to Les. 'Open it at page 196.'

The book was a cheap, second-hand paperback — *The Changing Society Of China* by Ch'u Chai and Winberg Chai. Page 196 opened at 'Kang Yu-Wei And The Reform Movement'. Underneath that it said, 'Kang's Political Views and Activities'. Beneath that, however, a square space had been cut out of the pages and sitting snugly in the space was a programme data disk. Norton picked it carefully from inside the book and turned it over in his hand.

'Do you know what that it, Les?'

'Yeah, it's a floppy disk for a computer. But, hey, Garrick, as far as computers go, I know what one looks like and that's about it.'

'All right. Fair enough,' nodded the major. 'Anyway, Les, I found this on the floor this morning, so I put it through Ackerley's computer and I got those ten pages of print sitting on the table.'

'And just what did you find out, Major?'

'Well, for starters, I found out the truth about Ackerley.'

'Susie said he was a student or something. Writing a book.'

The major shook his head. 'He's a young journalist. His name's Mark Prior and he comes from Geelong in Victoria.'

'Fair dinkum?'

The Gecko looked at Les for a moment. 'This friend of yours — Susie — has she got a real lot of brains?'

Norton shrugged. 'She's got her street smarts, but she's no rocket scientist.'

The Gecko nodded. 'Yeah, this bloke's probably lobbed here because it's handy for his research, plus he needed a place where he could come and go or piss off if he wanted to. And I'd say Susie needed the money to help pay the rent.'

'Yeah, that'd be about right,' agreed Les. 'So what's this Prior bloke up to? He hasn't been murdered or something, has he?'

The Gecko gave a quick shake of his head. 'No. He's out gathering more research. That's why he took his small radio and left his computer. I think he's up on the Central Coast.'

'All right. So what's he up to, Major? What have you got there?'

The major picked up the sheets of paper. 'What I've got here, Les, is a data printout. Now, it's full of techno-jargon and transformed code lines and references to other text files and data merges. And there's another programme data disk somewhere with all Prior's information or story on it. But basically, Les, to put it in layman's terms, this is a synopsis or hypothesis of his theory.'

Norton was lost already. 'Sir Noposis? Wasn't he a knight of the round table?'

'Very funny, Les. All right, I'll make it simpler again. In a nutshell — this is a nutshell of what he is working on.'

'And what was he working on, Major?'

The Gecko looked evenly at Les. 'Prior was onto a conspiracy behind the death of Harold Holt.'

'Harold Holt?' Norton's eyebrows knitted. 'The Australian Prime Minister who drowned in . . .'

'December 1967, Les. Disappeared, presumed drowned, off Cheviot Beach in Victoria. I remember it well.' The Gecko tapped the ten pages of print. 'I've gone through this three times, Les. Prior hasn't quite found the body — yet. But it all makes sense and this young journo's sources of information and his contacts are spot on. Spot . . . on.'

'All right, Major,' nodded Les, 'so in a nutshell, what's this conspiracy about Harold doing a "Harold" in 1967?'

'In a nutshell, Les,' The Gecko looked at the papers then back to Les, 'according to Prior, Harold Holt was a Chinese spy and the KGB shot him under orders from ASIO.'

Norton gave a double blink. 'Shit! That's pretty heavy stuff, Major.'

The Gecko tapped the pages again. 'This is a pretty heavy story, Les.'

'Fuckin' hell!'

'You want to hear it?'

'Yeah, all right. What happened?'

'Okay. Now we all know Harold Holt was born in Sydney on 5 August, 1905 . . .' While the major spoke, he'd refer to the papers occasionally, but mostly he talked as if he were relating the story from memory. He spoke slowly and carefully, however, and somehow Les was able to get the picture. 'His first school was Abbotsholme College in Killara, then Wesley College in Victoria, and Queens College in Melbourne where he studied for his law degree. But we won't dwell on all that. We'll fast forward to 1929 to the William Quick Club at Queens College where young Harold earned a reputation as a debater and an orator. In fact, he won the Oratory Medal in 1929 and was the Queens champion in the debating field. But for some reason, Holt had this mad affection for China and the Chinese people.'

'He did?'

'Yeah. He even wrote this paper called "Hands Off China" and delivered it at the William Quick Club, where it caused a bit of a sensation. Not only for the fervour with which he delivered it, but because it was considered to be very left-wing at the time. The government and mood of the day was very conservative, the White Australia policy was firmly in place and the Chinese were aligned more with Russia — the dreaded Soviet Union. But the paper tore strips off the British and the United States. A Chinese delegate in the audience, Chu Yu-lan, liked it so much, he invited Holt round to the Consulate-General in William Street for tea, where they bought the paper off him for thirty guineas, which was a fair bit of money in those days.'

'It is now,' said Les.

'True enough, lad. Anyway, the inscrutable orientals asked Holt if he had any more complimentary things he wanted to say about China or articles he wanted to write and Holt couldn't deliver them fast enough. So, through Chu Yu-lan, they bought them off him, paying him generously in cash, steadily roping him in, and by keeping an inscrutable eye on him, Chu also found the Chinese had another thing going for them. As well as a good debate, young law student Harold liked a game of cards — mainly poker — at a place in Melbourne called the Green Room, where young Harold, like his inscrutable Chinese friends, had a reputation for bluff and a perfect poker face. You know what I mean by that, Les?'

'Hey, Garrick, you're talking to a bloke that works in a casino.'

'Of course, Les. I forgot. So everybody was happy. The Chinese knew Holt was a young man going places and they had him right in, along with his articles. Holt was rapt about being on such good terms with his favourite people and he had plenty of money left over to play poker with.' The major ran his finger down one of the pages. 'Prior's got all the dates down here. The amounts of money. Other names — Liao-Chi, Sheng Nung. There's even a reference to Harold's favourite uncle, F. W. Eggleston, who was the Victorian Attorney-General in the 1920s and finished up being Australia's first diplomatic minister in China.'

'Was he a spy too?' asked Les.

'No, only Harold, who's now in fairly deep with the Kuomintang government in Nanking under Chiang Kai-shek, up to the Japanese invasion of Manchuria in 1931, Mao Tse-tung's start of the Long March in 1934 and the full-scale Japanese invasion in 1937, the start of the Second World War and so on. But, even though

Holt was still only in his early thirties and still considered a sleeper as much as a spy, it'll tell you how much the Chinese valued him. We'll fast forward again to 1941. Holt's the Member for Fawkner and a backbencher in parliament, and not all that happy being a backbencher. He has a fight with Prime Minister Menzies and quits parliament to join the AIF as a gunner. Rather than risk him being killed in the war, the Chinese get one of their agents, Chou Fung-yi, to plant a bomb on a plane in Canberra that crashes, killing three government ministers, including Jeffrey Street, the Minister for Defence. So Menzies has to slide Holt straight back into the cabinet as Minister for Labour and National Service.'

'Shit!'

'So now the Chinese have got a full-blown spy right in the middle of the Australian government. And it all started with a young student delivering a paper on China at a university debate.' The Gecko deflected to the papers for a moment. 'But, by now, Harold's starting to come under a bit of pressure. With the war raging against Japan, all Asians in Australia are under suspicion, so it's not so easy for Holt to be seen in the company of too many Chinese. Plus there was a bit of smut and innuendo being bantered around parliament by the Labor Party. One particularly fierce exchange between Holt and the Labor Party is recorded in Hansard. Then on top of that, Mao Tse-tung's communists kicked Chiang Kai-shek's Nationalists out of China onto Taiwan. However, Chu Yu-lan defected to the communists and was able to slot Holt in easily enough, so it was business as usual. But, shit, you can

184

imagine the pressure he was under. A member of a right-wing government spying for the communists and all this other business going on around him.' Norton nodded. 'Anyway, we'll brush all that and fast forward it again to June 1950 and the Korean War, where Holt really came into his own as a spy. In fact Holt's spying for the Chinese was that good. He inadvertently helped bring the Korean War to an early end.'

'Hawkeye Pearce and Major Winchester would have loved him.'

'Yeah, right. Anyway, according to Prior, along with everything else he was telling the Chinese, Holt mentioned he heard that a bunch of red-neck Republicans were lobbying in Congress to bomb the shit right out of China if the armistice negotiations failed, starting with their bases on the Korean border, then right up to Peking. And if that didn't work, they'd nuke them. So the Chinese eased up. Even if the war did drag on as a police action till 1953.'

'Giving us another 500 episodes of "M.A.S.H.".'

'True, Les. But Holt did get a concession from the Chinese. Go easy on the Australian troops in Korea. And the Chinese agreed to do their best. Australian casualties were considered light in Korea. There's more here about the Malaysia Campaign. Suez Canal. Even the Mau Mau in Africa. Harold earned his money. But what about this, Les? Since 1945, the Russians knew what Holt was up to. The Chinese knew the Russians knew, but didn't tell Holt.'

'How did the Russians find out?'

'Early up, Australia didn't have a CIA or MI5 — a Secret Service. So ASIO was set up during the war years. But unbeknown to the government, one member of British Intelligence it brought out to help get ASIO going — Roderick Collins — was a KGB agent. He went to Cambridge with Philby, Burgess and McLean. The Russians had turned him and he never got caught from day one. He knew Holt was a spy from one of his contacts in the Kuomintang, Wu Tao-pang, and Collins didn't particularly like Holt over an incident at a British Embassy dinner. Holt punched him.'

'The PM put one on the pommy mug. Unreal! What for?'

'Over a Chinese waitress at the party. Evidently Harold didn't mind a bit of Asian snatch on the side, too, if he could get it. So Holt goes spying along not knowing he's got an enemy in the camp, biding his time. Anyway, Les, we'll fast forward again into the Vietnam War. Holt's high up in Cabinet giving the Chinese the times when the B52 strikes would come over. American troop movements. Armaments. But once again he got a concession to go easy on the Australian soldiers. The VC wouldn't agree to this at first, but eventually figured the Australians weren't Americans and were that much trouble anyway, they engaged them as little as possible.' The Gecko smiled at Les. 'We used to give 'em shit, if they wanted to come looking for it.'

'I imagine you would, Major,' said Les.

'Anyway, the Vietnam War's raging, Holt's doing his best to get it together, and on January 20, 1966, Menzies throws the towel in and Harold Holt becomes Prime Minister of Australia. Holt's a bit spun out, but it's congratulations all round and the Chinese decide to

186

do the right thing and tell Holt about Collins. They do it through a Russian agent, Oleg Vatutin. Holt wasn't to know they knew. Vatutin was friends with Holt. They both liked a drink and a laugh. Played poker. Holt nicknamed Oleg, Ollie, and considered Vatutin a bit of a joker. They used to go skindiving and spearfishing together. So Vatutin, as a friend, told Holt about Collins. There was nothing he could do. Don't mention he'd told him. On top of just becoming Prime Minister this was the ultimate pressure Holt didn't need.'

'I'm surprised at the balls he had to get this far.'

'About now Collins decides to strike. Cut the new Prime Minister right off at the knees. He arranges for a private meeting in his office with Holt and tells the PM he knows what's going on. Holt says he knows what's going on too. How were your days at Cambridge? Here's a photo of you and your school chums. So it's a kind of stalemate. Though Collins did have one advantage. If Holt called first. Collins could defect to Russia. There was nowhere for Holt to go if he had to face the music. Only gaol.'

'So Harold's got troubles.'

'Right. The shit's finally hit the fan. Plus, after thirty years of spying and the pressure involved, his verandah's starting to get a few loose floorboards. So he thinks it over and decides to bail out. He tells Collins he's won. But he won't blow Collins' cover and Collins can stay in Australia with ASIO if he'll ensure that Holt gets out of the country safely and secretively. Collins agrees. So Holt, with the help of the Chinese, Oleg Vatutin and ASIO, arrange a plan. The Prime Minister would disappear while skindiving. A Chinese

Whiskey-class submarine, with divers on board, would pick the Prime Minister up, then take him to a remote island off the south of China where Harold would spend the rest of his days amongst the people he liked most, skindiving and porking young Chinese babes with no shortage of money in the bank. Not a bad idea and much better than the alternative. They set it all up, including a contingency plan, and the whole lot stuffed up completely.'

'What happened?'

'They arranged for the submarine to pick Holt up off Cheviot Beach. Holt had a weekender near the water and used to spend a lot of time diving and entertaining there. You have to remember, Les, this was Australia in 1967. Cheviot Beach was, like, out in the bush, people had their minds on the Vietnam War and the protests and half our naval patrol boats were either over there or on manoeuvres. There was no satellite surveillance or navigation like today and you could pull something like that off then. Collins arranged for all Holt's usual security staff to have the day off. Vatutin would be in a Holden panel van up above the cliffs with another KGB operative, Vasily Khludov. Sitting further along the cliffs in another car, was another Russian agent, Pavel Yusupov. He was a lot younger and fitter than Holt, had the same build, the same clothes on, with a thick, grey wig in the car, and he was to double for Holt or distract people's attention if something went wrong. Harold arranged for a small party of friends to be there for a day's snorkelling. Holt would drive himself to the cliffs on top of the beach, leave his car, then walk down with his diving gear and join his friends.

Then he'd jump in the water, the Chinese divers would be waiting with an aqua-lung for him and they'd swim him out to the submarine, and that should have been that. Exit the prime minister, stage left.'

'So what went wrong?'

'First, the seas came up. There'd been a bad swell running, but on that particular Sunday, it was huge. It would be hard enough for the experienced Chinese divers with scuba gear to get in. For a man in his sixties, who wasn't as fit as he used to be, to jump into those seas, he'd risk drowning. On top of that, Sir Alec Rose, the round-the-world yachtsman, arrived in his boat *The Lively Lady*. This was a big event and thousands of people converged on Portsea that day, along with the Water Police and units of the Australian Navy. Naturally all boats were equipped with the latest radar. The submarine couldn't risk being detected so, it was mission aborted. Go to plan two. The submarine would head for Port Stephens near Newcastle and pick the Prime Minister up there, but Holt still has to go through with all the subterfuge. So he joins his friends walking across the beach, then halfway across, excuses himself for a minute while he runs over behind some rocks near an old upturned fishing boat to change into his Speedos. Prior's even mentioned how one woman in Holt's party remarked at the inquest on the Prime Minister's sudden touch of modesty. Usually he'd just drop his daks on the spot. And, apart from them, there was hardly anyone else around. It just seemed a little unusual at the time. So Holt runs over behind the rocks where Yusupov is waiting with the wig on. The Russian takes Holt's snorkelling gear, then runs back down to Holt's friends, keeps away from them a bit, then, with a bit of the old "last one in's a rotten egg" sort of thing, runs down to the water, jumps in and swims out. Holt puts on a dark cap Yusupov has left him, waits a few minutes till everyone's down by the water's edge, then runs up the hill to where Oleg and Vasily are parked next to an old gun turret. Holt gets in the back of the panel van and they head for Port Stephens to wait for the submarine. Yusupov swims around for a while, then takes the grey wig off, swims back in and hides in the rocks for a little while longer. Later, in all the confusion, he walks calmly up to his car and drives off. And that, too, should have been that, except they got sprung.'

'They got sprung? Who by?'

'A bloke having a root under the old, upturned fishing boat.'

'You're kidding?'

'Just above Cheviot Beach is an Officer Cadet Training School. A young Lieutenant there, Kenneth Trenowden, was having an affair with the Commanding Officer's wife, while he was posted to Vietnam. The old fishing boat was their Sunday rendezvous point where they used to do their bonking in private. Trenowden was giving her one under the boat when, first he heard noises, then a familiar voice. He kept the CO's wife quiet while he had a look out through a hole in the clinkers and saw the whole thing. Holt actually caught his eye for an instant before he ran up the hill. Naturally, the young lieutenant was blown out by what he just saw, but he can't tell anybody or it would be the end of his career, amongst other things. So he kept the whole thing to himself. However, he did write a letter, a sort of "in the event of my death" thing, and left it with his sister, Beverley. Two weeks later, Trenowden got a posting to Vietnam where he was shot by a sniper at My Phuoc Tuy. Very coincidental. His sister forgot about the letter and ended up moving to Geelong when her husband retired. He later electrocuted himself trying to fix a power point. When she was going through her private papers after it was all over, she found the letter from her dead brother, read it and gave it to Prior. He was her nephew and she knew he was a journalist. He's read it, got a bit suss about this uncle getting knocked off in Vietnam so early when he shouldn't really have got the posting. He revved up his modem, jumped on the internet, and zoomed off gathering information from all over the world on the super-highway, whereas, unfortunately, Les, you're in an old Holden sitting on blocks with no wheels.'

'Okay, I'm a loo-light or a loo-dite. Or whatever you call them. But you still haven't told me what happened to the Prime Minister's body?'

'Okay, sit back, Br'er Rabbit, and ol' Uncle Remus'll finish this off for you. Phase Two. The panel van heads for Port Stephens. They hide Holt in a caravan near Shoal Bay, but Williamtown Air Force Base is just up the road and the SAS are having parachute exercise droppings into Port Stephens. The Australian Navy's doing mine sweeping operations along with two American destroyers prior to leaving for Vietnam, plus the Air Force is doing low-level bombing exercises and submarine detection. So it's mission aborted again. Plan Three. Sydney Heads. But by now the light's stopped coming on in Harold's fridge. He's starting to crack. Oleg does his best to boost the PM's morale and crack gags and joke around. But Harold's losing it. They move into a flat in Rose Bay. Oleg organises a drink and a game of poker to keep Holt's mind off things. He gets drunk and sees himself on TV. The whole country's still looking for him. Then it flashes to his family all crying and praying, and Harold goes all lachrymose and decides to give himself up. He'll cop the rap. Holt's good Russian mate, Vatutin, rings Collins and asks what to do? And Collins said to shoot the Prime Minister. So Vatutin did, just like that.' The Gecko snapped his fingers twice and looked at Les.

'His Russian mate shot him?'

'Yep, twice in the back of the neck — SS style.'

'So where's the body?'

'Well, Les, that's where the story ends. Or splits into two. The Chinese said they picked up the body, took it to China and buried it. But another report said the submarine got caught in fishing nets off North Head, burnt a motor out getting away from them, and headed out to sea for repairs, then back to China. Vatutin said they disposed of the body in his report. Khludov said there was a mishap with the body, but they disposed of it. That's all. Prior's got some longitude and latitude references there. I haven't got the gizmo with me, but by memory they seem to be around Brisbane Water.'

'Up the Central Coast.'

'Possibly. And that's where Prior is at the moment. He might be onto something.'

'Funny if he was under the Florida Hotel,' laughed Norton.

'I think that's gone now, Les. It's Crown Plaza, or something.'

'Is it? It's a while since I been up there.'

The Gecko eased back in his seat and gave Norton a slow smile. 'Well, come on, Les. What are your thoughts on Prior's theory? You must have formed some sort of an opinion.'

'Yeah, not bad,' nodded Les. 'But there are just a couple of things.'

'Like what, lad?'

'Well, why would Holt keep going? Once he got into parliament, he didn't need the money, especially when he made Prime Minister.'

'Holt still needed money. As well as poker and a punt, he liked the high life in general. And he was Prime Minister for barely a year. But when you're in there, you don't think of the circumstances. It's the buzz. I was in Army Intelligence. I've worked with spies. They're ice-cold adrenalin junkies getting high on controlled schizophrenia. Plus Holt believed in what he was doing. In his heart and soul, he honestly believed he was doing the right thing. The way things are coming out now with generals and ministers spilling their guts, possibly he was.'

'Okay,' nodded Les, 'that makes sense. But how did Prior get onto all this in the first place? I know he's a journalist, and he can use a computer . . .'

'Like I said, Les. On the internet. It's all out there now. Since the break-up of Russia, the wall coming down and the end of the Cold War, there's records turning up everywhere. Vatutin ended up a colonel in the Stasi, the East German Secret Police, along with

Khludov's son, Lieutenant Nevsky Khludov. Vasily died flying a plane during the start of the war in Afghanistan. Chu Yu-lan is now number three in the Chinese Politburo. Prior's been researching this for almost four years and knows what he's doing. He's done six trips overseas, including Moscow and Beijing.' The Gecko patted the ten pages. 'It's all there, mate. Have a look for yourself.'

'No, that's okay. I'll take your word for it.' With all the techno-jargon in it, Norton may as well have tried to read a Chinese newspaper. 'But it's not as good as the theory I heard. From very reliable sources, too, I might add.'

'What theory was that, Les?'

'Harold Holt and Elvis Presley are running a fish and chip shop with Spike Milligan at Woy Woy.'

The Gecko was about to say something when the intercom buzzed. 'Shit! That'll be Eddie. Don't say anything about this.' He gathered the papers up. 'I'll go through it with him some other time.' The major hit the intercom, put the papers in his room and was at the front door in time to open it for Eddie, who was wearing jeans, dark blue T-shirt, cap and sunglasses.

Eddie smiled when he walked into the kitchen. 'So, how's it goin', big fellah? You ready for all the festivities tonight?'

'Ready as I'll ever fuckin' be, Eddie, I suppose. What about you?'

Eddie made an expression with his hands. 'What's gotta be done's gotta be done.'

'Yeah, I s'pose you're right. You want a cup of coffee or something?'

194

'Yeah, all right. Thanks, mate.' Eddie looked across at the major. 'So what's been happening, Garrick? Everything sweet?'

The Gecko made the same expression with his hands that Eddie had. 'What could go wrong?'

'Listen,' said Les, 'if you two want to go in the lounge. I'll make this and bring it in.'

'That would be excellent, Les. There are things I have to discuss. Thank you.'

Well, here I am, the little au-pair girl again. And once again I've learnt something from the major. I've learnt that I know absolutely fuck-all about computers and he's a whiz. I don't know about Prior, or whatever he calls himself's, story. But the major's a genius — how he got onto it and figured it all out. So Harold's buried somewhere near Brisbane Water, eh, and there was a mishap with the body. A sobering thought suddenly hit Norton in the pit of his stomach. Just as long as there's no bloody mishap with two certain bodies tonight. Les stared out the kitchen window into space. I honestly wish I didn't have to do this. For some reason I'm starting to get a bad feeling. Oh well, too bloody late now. He had all the stuff together on the tray and was just about to pick up the plunger from near the kitchen sink when Boris and Igor came out the front door and walked down the path towards the front of the flats. Off for another day's fishing, are we, boys? Les let his eyes follow them for a moment, then he took the tray into the lounge, placed it all in front of Eddie, then walked out onto the sundeck and made out he was looking for something. The two Russians had gone past the front of the flats and were almost at

Glenayr Avenue when two fresh-faced, fit-looking young blokes came out of the flats opposite where Les had seen the outline of the telephoto lens. One had bright red hair, the other black, and both were wearing Hawaiian shirts, board shorts and sunglasses, and were carrying boogie-boards under their arms. Something about their outfits told you they were anything but surfers. Les pottered around watching them for a while, then went back inside.

'Those two Russians just went down the road and two blokes came out of that block of flats opposite. I think they were following them,' he said to the major.

'That doesn't surprise me,' replied the major. 'Were they dressed as surfers?'

'Yeah.'

'Look like it, don't they.'

'Like anything but. They worth worrying about?'

The Gecko shook his head. 'No. They're after Boris and Igor for some reason. Probably like what I said.'

'Is there some drama?' asked Eddie, over the top of his coffee.

'No,' reiterated the major, 'nothing to do with us.'

'Good.' Eddie looked up at Norton. 'Sit down and have a cuppa, Les. And I'll tell you what's going on again. It's simple really.'

'Righto.' Les sat down facing Eddie and the major and got a cup of coffee together. 'Give me the SITCOM. Let's get this briefing together.'

'Okay, old boy,' replied Eddie, starting off with a mock British accent. 'Here's the poop. The gen. You and Garrick are going to blow the handball court at ten.

But first you leave your car above the boatsheds at Ben Buckler and walk round. When the bang goes up, I'll arrive in a rubber ducky. We'll toss the bodies into the rubber ducky and take them out to a fishing boat and they'll take them out to sea and dump them. Then I take you back to the boatsheds and you run Garrick into Central railway to catch the train home. A piece of cake, old boy.'

'Yeah, easy as shit. Just blow up half the baths, grab a couple of stiffs, throw them in a dinghy, and take them out to another boat for a burial at sea. What about this atom bomb he's using? It'll probably light up all Bondi Bay and half of Dover Heights.'

'Only for a second or two, Les,' said the major. 'And there might be a bit of noise, but nothing to worry about. Hey, trust me, Les. I haven't let you down yet, have I?'

'No, I don't suppose so,' replied Norton reluctantly.

'But what about this for a stroke of genius, Les,' said Eddie. 'The caretaker's at work tonight. And because of the council, the club stops trading at eight. I'm going down there with a spray can when they close and writing HANDS OFF THE BERGS. DEATH TO THE ZIONIST DOGS. AL FATAH on the wall opposite.'

'Why the bloody hell's that?' asked Les.

'There's a rumour going round that the Jews have bought the baths for development. With that plastered all over the wall, it'll look like the work of Arab terrorists. Grouse or what, Les?'

Les shook his head. 'Terrific. And who's going to be in the rubber ducky with you? Who's driving the getaway car? Or fishing boat?'

Eddie rubbed his hands together. 'I got a couple of surprises for you — you'll love it.'

'I can't wait.'

'So that's the story, Les. Garrick's got all the times and exact locations written down. After the explosion we should be away in five minutes. Eight max.' Eddie drained his coffee and stood up. 'Anyway, I got to piss off. I got other things to organise. So everything's about right, Garrick?' he said to the major.

'Everything's fine, Eddie. I can't see one hitch. I'll make the device this afternoon and prime it. We do the job at ten. And around ten the next morning I'll be home with my loving family. Beautiful.'

'All right,' said Eddie. 'I'll see you at the baths tonight. I can let myself out. See you, fellahs. And good luck.'

'Yeah, see you, Eddie,' chorused Les and the major. The door closed and Eddie was gone.

Les finished his coffee also and looked at the major. 'So what's our story now, Major?'

'Well,' answered The Gecko, looking at his watch, 'by the time we clean this up and I get a few things sorted out, it'll be lunchtime, and I wouldn't mind another of those chicken schnitzels. That was good yesterday.'

'Okay. I'm starting to feel a bit peckish now myself.'

'Then we might go and walk it off.'

'Walk it off,' echoed Norton.

The Gecko smiled at Les. 'You heard what I said, Les. Of course, you don't have to come if you don't wish.'

'No, I'll come,' said Les, just a trifle reluctantly.

'Good lad.'

Which was pretty much how they spent the afternoon. Les fiddled round in his room, still a bit apprehensive. Despite his assurances, Eddie made it all sound too easy. All Les did know was the major found a CD amongst Susie's collection — Andrew Denton's 'The Money Or The Gun' with twenty-two versions of 'Stairway To Heaven', including one by The Beatnix. The Gecko found it, and the remote, and played it non-stop until they left for the Bondi No Names. The food was excellent again. Except that when the waitress asked Les if he enjoyed his meal, instead of answering her, he turned to the major and said, 'There's a sign on the door, but she wants to be sure, because you know sometimes words have two meanings'.

Their walk afterwards started off pretty punishing; Norton's legs were still stiff from the day before. But fortunately the major showed mercy at the stairs, saying there was no sense risking an injury with what they had in front of them that night. So they only went up and down twice. Back at the unit they got cleaned up and Les was standing in the lounge room in his shorts and a blue T-shirt when the major came out wearing his tracksuit pants and an old grey T-shirt.

'Okay, Les,' he said, 'I'm going to be working on this for the next couple of hours. Why don't you continue with your taping? I'd rather it if you stayed here in the flat.'

'Suits me, Major. Can I help you in any way?'

The Gecko stared at Les for a moment. 'Do you know anything about titanium steel alloy? Mini

calutronic particle accelerators? Lithium and plutonium catalystic neutron blizzards?'

Les stared back at the major for a moment. 'I'm not
bad on particle accelerators, but I'd need the manual
for the other stuff.'

'Stay here and tape your music, Les. I'll see you in
a couple of hours.' The Gecko went to his room and
closed the door.

Lithium and plutonium fuckin' what? Les shook his
head. Oh well, mine is not to reason why, mine is but
to tape or die. He unwrapped another cassette and
started going through Susie's CDs again. The first two
tracks Les taped were 'Communication Breakdown'
by Flash and the Pan and 'Good Good Good' by The
Cockroaches. Two hours later he'd finished one tape
and had started another. He stretched his back and
walked out onto the verandah. It was almost dark.
There were a few people coming and going and car
headlights going past, but no sign of anybody Les
knew. When he came inside the major was standing in
the lounge room rubbing his eyes and stretching his
neck.

'How are you feeling, Major. Everything okay?'
asked Norton.

'Yes, Les,' replied the major. 'Everything's A1. As
good as I can possibly get it.'

'Your eyes look a bit sore.'

'Yes, I've been peering through a magnifying glass
half the afternoon. I'm going to make a cup of tea. Do
you want one?'

'No, you go for your life, mate. I'll knock this on the
head.' Les finished the last track he was taping, 'She

Moved The Dishes First' by Supercharge, and sat down on the lounge. The Gecko came out of the kitchen holding a mug with a teabag string hanging down the side. He looked down at Norton.

'Well, would you like to see what I've been up to all afternoon, Les?'

'Yeah, sure. Show us your atom bomb, Major. Long as the bloody thing doesn't go off and blow us into the harbour.'

'You'd simply vapourise, Les. In less than a micro-second.'

The Gecko went to his room and returned with his 'atom bomb'. It was a brown, curved plastic object about 18 inches long, 10 inches wide and 3 inches thick, sitting at an angle on four spindly, pointed metal legs. On one side was written FRONT TOWARD ENEMY, on the other side, BACK, and beneath that 14-33 APERS MINE. Beneath that was the serial number, Lot MHK71A631-001. There were two plastic mouldings on top with threaded ends something like a tap. A brown cable ran to a roll of cable on the floor and sitting next to it was a flat plastic object with a moveable top that held a fat, round firing button inside. Another smaller box was attached to the front with thick cables and covers something like those on a distributor cap.

'So that's it, eh?' said Les.

'Basically. All it is is a Claymore mine. Except instead of ball-bearings and shrapnel spraying out the front, there'll be a small, fully contained thermal fire-ball — only blue with orange tints. They're quite pretty really. There'll be some noise and a few shockwaves for a moment. Nothing bad. Then that side of the handball court and the wall will look as if it's been whipped out like a scoop of ice-cream, only with pumice flavouring. It might get a bit dusty too. So bring a hankie or something to put over your face.'

'What about radioactivity?'

'Nothing to worry about. I'm only using cooked-up, spent uranium, and what there is'll get blown away. But wash your clothes and have a good shower later if you want to.'

'I think I'll be having a long shower.'

'Well, that's about it. All we can do now is sit around and wait till it's time to go. You got some dark clothes you can wear tonight, Les?'

'Yeah. I got some stuff in my bag.'

'Okay, then why don't we sit around, watch a bit of TV and relax. You're not hungry are you, Les?' Norton shook his head. 'We might make some coffee and toast later, and be ready to leave by nine.'

'All right,' agreed Les. 'Sounds good to me.'

'Cybill' and 'Murphy Brown' were funny. They had half a pot of coffee and some toast and were watching something about Russia on SBS when Les drifted into his room to see what was in his bag — something dark and something he didn't need. His jeans were dark enough and he had his black grunge boots. He'd also tossed in a long-sleeved black T-shirt he'd bought when he was drunk at a Meat Balls 'Fat Out Of Hell' concert one night. And a dark blue bushmaster jacket George Brennan had conned him into buying at the club on another night. It was brand-new and had pockets and velcro catches all over it. But it was two sizes too big and you could have hidden a side of beef in it.

Les got into his outfit, looked in the mirror and shook his head. I look like Matt Helm wearing a life-jacket. He had one last look around Susie's room, then turned the light out and went into the lounge room. The Gecko was standing in front of his bags wearing black sneakers, blue tracksuit pants, a black T-shirt and the same jacket he had on at the station.

'Nice outfit, Les. I see you're a Thomas Cook man, too.'

'I wouldn't wear anything else, Garrick.'

The Gecko looked at Les for a moment or two and he was definitely smiling. 'Well, Les,' he said, 'I don't quite know how to say this, but, this is it — you've been great to be on board with, and I'd like to offer you my hand. I hope everything goes to plan tonight.'

'Yeah, let's hope so, Garrick. I have to tell you, though, it wasn't quite the five days I had planned.'

Les offered his hand and both men shook warmly and sincerely.

'Now if you'd like to give me a hand with some of this, we'll get going.'

The Gecko picked up a blue canvas bag. Les picked up his bag and overnight bag.

'Well, at least you don't need your crutch now, Major. That's one good thing.'

'Yes, lad,' replied the major. 'I certainly don't need it now. But I'll keep it just the same. You never know when my ankle might go on me again.'

Les hit the security buttons and turned out the lights, then they went down to the garage. Les got the car out, then put the major's bags in the back, while he sat in the front holding the blue canvas bag. Les hit the button for the garage gate and they cruised up the side into Hall Street and headed for the boatsheds at Ben Buckler.

Not a great deal was said during the short drive from Hall Street down to Campbell Parade, then Ramsgate Avenue. Les was hoping the bomb wouldn't go off in the major's lap and he was concentrating on something, though the major did say something about how he had two hand grenades with him in case some rubble needed shifting, and that he usually fired these bombs by remote control, but seeing as there were so many mobile phones, electronic garage doors, two-way radios and whatever else in the area, he was using cable, so they might have to get a bit closer to the explosion than usual. But it was nothing to worry about. No, nothing to worry about, mused Les, as they parked in the small reserve above the big rock at Ben Buckler. I've always wanted to be standing at ground-zero when an atom bomb goes off.

The half moon slipped behind one of the numerous cloud banks crowding the night sky when they got out of the car. The air was somewhat humid and thick and a light southerly was tossing a few white horses across the inky blue water of Bondi Bay and a small choppy swell was washing unevenly against the shoreline. Traffic lights cruising up and down Campbell Parade seemed to blend in with the lights from the surrounding shops and buildings, melding in turn with the other buzz of street noise, and at the opposite end of the bay, the few remaining lights of Bondi baths and the Icebergs seemed to twinkle forlornly in the distance. It was definitely an ideal night to bomb an old building.

Les took the major's bags from the back of the utility and put them on the floor in the front of the car. Ben Buckler was a secluded area of Bondi and it was Friday night, so there was a good chance the bags'd be gone when they came back, along with the tonneau cover. Norton made sure the car was locked, the major picked up his blue canvas bag and they walked down Ramsgate Avenue to Bondi promenade.

They didn't say a great deal walking along the promenade either, it was well lit up and there was no shortage of people around. Couples arm in arm or hand in hand, kids on roller blades and bikes, others in small gangs either looking for trouble or hoping trouble would find them. Above the promenade on Queen Elizabeth Drive you could hear the pounding boom-boom-boom of house music pumping out of the suburbanite hoons' cars either prowling up the Drive or parked nose against the railing. This caused Norton to flippantly remark to the major that, no matter how loud his bomb was, you'd be flat out hearing it amongst the thumping disco banality filling the air. The Gecko flippantly agreed. They reached the end of the promenade, then followed the path up to the steps near the toilet block that would lead them, together, into Notts Avenue for the last time. The baths were softly lit and naturally deserted, but as they approached the front door to the Icebergs the first thing they noticed splattered against the wall opposite was HANDS OF THE BERGS. DEATH TO THE ZIONIST DOGS. AL FATAH. You couldn't miss it, even at night. It was bright red in letters about two metres high. Les imagined Eddie must have used a stepladder to put it up there.

'Nice to see Eddie's done his bit for multicultural-ism,' remarked Norton.

'Yeah. It's a pity he can't spell,' replied the major.

Three or four cars were sitting under the streetlights when they reached the end of Notts Avenue and the same lights cast a milky yellow pall over the slope leading down to the handball court. The major had an instinctive look around, then gave Les a nod and they started climbing down the sandy trail to the back way into the baths.

There was a slight swell bumping against the shore-line and, although that end of the beach was more sheltered against the southerly, a fine mist of salty spray hung in the warm night air as they carefully hopped from one rock to the next in the darkness. The pool where Eddie would bring the rubber ducky in was about half full and swirling around noticeably with the tide, but Les couldn't see him having any trouble get-ting it in; just as long as they could get it back out again with the extra passengers, alive *and* deceased. As they passed it, they both had another instinctive look around, then scampered quickly over the remaining rocks, past the pumphouse, then up the short set of steps and straight into the back of the handball court. It was just as dirty and still stank of their piss from last time they were in there. Only now it was a gloomy darkness, with barely enough light to cast a shadow.

'Okay, Les,' said the major, keeping his voice down. 'You don't have to do anything. Just keep an eye out, that's all.'

'Righto.' Les looked around and began wishing he was somewhere else.

The Gecko placed the blue canvas bag under the shelter next to the two meter boxes and unzipped it, taking out a small torch which he placed in his vest pocket. The mine was wrapped in a small thermal blanket with its legs folded underneath; he placed that beside the bag. Next was the spool of cable and the trigger housing, which he placed on the ground near to the mine. The Gecko then stood up and walked over to the handball court and the wall where he moved the beam from the torch around as if he was looking for something or making some last calculation. While he was looking around and watching the major, Les suddenly got this feeling someone was watching him. Les always had a sixth sense, which had developed working on the door when you're trying to stay a couple of lengths in front of the trouble, and it hit him right in the pit of his stomach. Except for his eyes swivelling round, Norton stood stock still as he tried to fathom the situation. They were both definitely being watched. Two small red dots just above the floor beneath the shelter caught Les's eye. He watched, transfixed, in the darkness for a second or two. Next thing a shiny black rat about as big as a Shetland pony leapt off the bench, hit the ground with a squeal and galloped over Norton's feet, straight out the entrance where they'd come in.

'Ohh shit!!' he yelped.

'What's up?' hissed the major.

'A bloody rat just ran over my foot. Jesus!'

'A rat? Christ! I thought you'd been shot.' The Gecko muttered something and went back to what he was doing.

God! I don't like this, Les mumbled to himself, as his nerves settled down and he went back to keeping an eye on things. Rats, bombs, hand grenades, old bodies. I got a bad feeling about this, somehow. The major finished running his torch round the walls and that and appeared to be staring at something in the light at his feet. He bent down for a few moments, then stood up again and seemed to be deep in thought as if something was wrong. In the dark silence of the old handball court, this got Norton more than a bit concerned. All he wanted to do was get the job done and get out of the place.

'Everything all right, Major?' he enquired, trying to sound casual.

The Gecko continued to stare at the ground a moment more, then turned to Les. 'Someone's been in here today.'

Les stared down at the major's feet. There were chalk marks and notations on the green edge of the handball court, some of which had been scuffed out. 'Probably some blokes in here playing handball,' he suggested, 'or council building inspectors.'

'Yeah, you could be right.' The major glanced at his watch. 'Anyway, let's pull our fingers out. It's show-time.'

The Gecko put his torch back inside his vest, picked up the mine, placed it carefully on the ground next to where Les had seen the chalk marks, with a couple of old housebricks across the folded metal legs. From where Les was standing, it appeared to be angled slightly forward and down. The major then screwed the detonating cable into the lug on top and ran the cable out. He gave the mine another small adjustment, then walked back, put the thermal blanket in the bag and picked up the spool of cable and the firing mechanism.

'Here, Les,' he said. 'You take the bag while I run the cable out. We'll go up those stairs near where we came in.'

There was a narrow set of concrete stairs outside the entrance to the handball court that ran under the landing and up into the Icebergs Club. Les started walking towards the stairs, watching as The Gecko ran the cable out behind him and followed him up the stairs. About halfway up the steps, the major stopped.

'Okay. Just here'll do.'

Norton sat on one of the steps and noticed he was sweating. His heart also felt as if it was going to pound through his chest, while he drowned in the adrenalin that was squirting out of his stomach. Les had been a little nonchalant at times through the week, making jokes about what was going on. Now, this was it, the moment of truth; and no matter what might happen, there was no turning back. Whatever Norton's feelings, The Gecko ignored him. He clamped the cable into the firing mechanism and slid the top off. From his pocket he took two small ear-plugs and stuffed them in his ears, then looked at his watch on his left wrist while his right hand held the trigger. Les watched the back of his head in the gloom for a short while then his head seemed to nod slightly. Les stuffed his fingers in his own ears and closed his eyes tight just as The Gecko closed his right hand.

The hoons on the prom and just about every other citizen around the beachfront and beyond must have wondered what was going on. One minute there was just the usual street noise of cars and pumping techno music. Then a massive explosion shook all the surrounding windows, interrupted the music and rattled out across the bay like the crack of some monstrous tidal wave smashing down onto wet sand. This was followed by a huge blue fireball, tinged with red and orange, that lit up half the beachfront, as it rolled and tumbled like it was trying to devour itself before it blasted out from the back of the baths, sending half the handball court, the sea wall, concrete, rocks and anything else in its path splashing and spattering into the ocean. What didn't get blown out across the bay or up into the air tumbled down onto the rocks in front of where the handball court used to be. The flash vanished and the echo from the explosion faded, then a gigantic smoke ring spiralled up into the night sky through the settling dust and ash.

From where Les was sitting, it was like being trapped in an Otto bin before someone threw it down a lift shaft. Everything around him seemed to shake and the noise was unimaginable. Norton missed the blue fireball, but, even with his eyes jammed shut, it was as if someone had let off a flash camera next to his head. Then there was this awful silence.

'Righto, come on, Les, bring the bag. Let's go.'

The major's slightly muffled voice snapped Les back to life. He blinked his eyes open and noticed The Gecko had a hankie tied round his face; the one thing Les had forgotten to bring. 'Yeah, all right.'

Les picked up the bag and scrambled down the stairs after the major, who was winding up the cable as he went; arms and legs going at a hundred miles an hour.

They raced along the landing and into the handball court, or what was left of it. It was pretty much like the major had said. As if someone had taken out a giant scoop and flicked it out into the ocean. Where the handball court had been was a crater about two metres deep and about six metres across, leading out to sea where, if Les wasn't mistaken, a black rubber ducky was coming into view. Part of the wall into the handball court had been blown off, the fence and the far wall were down, and there was a fine dust settling over everything — something like volcanic ash. But where the sea wall and the handball court had been blown out, it almost formed a ramp down to the rockpool so, apart from the fine dust everywhere, getting the two bodies down to the rubber ducky wouldn't be much of a problem at all. The burnt-off end of the cable finished near the crater. The major wound the last of it up and handed the lot to Les.

'Put these in the bag, Les,' he said and jumped down into the crater. 'All we've got to do now is get these bodies and piss off.'

Les took the spool and stuffed it in the canvas bag. He was about to join the major when suddenly Les heard this odd scratching, scampering, squealing sound. He looked at the ash-covered floor and it was like a moving grey carpet. Cockroaches. Millions of them. Along with the relations of the rat Les had seen earlier and *their* relations. Whatever hadn't been nuked was heading for the nearest exit.

'Don't worry, Major. I'm right behind you.' Les stomped two fat ones that were just about to get on his boots and jumped in the dust-filled crater.

The Gecko was scuffing around on the floor of the crater with his foot. Les put the bag down and watched him as the fine, almost greasy, dust settled in his eyes, ears, nose, mouth, down his T-shirt and anywhere else he had an opening, like dry cement. As he was standing there watching The Gecko, Les heard another strange noise. A creaking, groaning sound, like some giant walking down a huge, old wooden staircase. It was weird and seemed to be coming from beneath him as well as around him. But sure enough, where the major had been scuffing with his foot, a slight hump was sticking out from the smooth floor of the crater that looked like dust-covered oilskin. Once again The Gecko hadn't ceased to amaze. He'd not only gauged the depth of the crater almost to the centimetre, all the surrounding soil and smashed concrete had been loosened up, so they'd have no trouble digging the bodies out as well. Les almost allowed himself a grim smile. Apart from being covered in dust, sweat, and all sorts of other shit in the air, and having cockroaches and rats crawling over him, it didn't look like it was turning out to be too bad a night. Les was about to comment on this to the major when the far side of the crater erupted in great plumes of dust and the angry whine of ricocheting bullets. Les didn't have to be told twice this time to pull his head down. He dived up against the opposite wall of the crater and tried to dig his way into it as another spray of bullets kicked up more dusty geysers about his head. Les heard the faint rattle of a bolt action and the clatter of spent casings landing on concrete and also didn't need to be told someone was firing a silenced automatic weapon at him. He turned to see the major had torn off his hankie and was burrowed up against the wall next to him.

'Major, what the fuck's goin' on?'

'Someone's up there with a machine gun,' answered the major. 'Two of them.'

'Not the bloody Mossad again?'

'I'm buggered if I know.'

Norton was about to say something, when Eddie Salita landed in the dust alongside them, his chest heaving up and down.

'What the fuck's goin' on?' he said, wiping ash from his eyes. 'They were bullets.'

'Someone up there's firing a bloody machine gun at us,' yelped Les.

The Gecko gave Eddie a very strange look. 'You never mentioned anything about this, Eddie,' he said, slowly and deliberately.

Eddie stared back at the major, then Les, then the major again. 'Don't ask me what's going on, but I suppose I'd better have a look.' Eddie pulled a Glock automatic pistol from out of a shoulder holster and edged cautiously up to the edge of the crater.

The firing seemed to be coming from the landing above the other side of the stairs where Les and the major took cover when the major let the bomb off. Another burst of fire tore up the top of the crater and Eddie was about to fire a few shots back when a voice hollered out from the landing at the other end of the baths.

'Government agents! Throw down your weapons!'

Eddie was incredulous. 'What'd he bloody say?'

Norton shrugged. 'FBI, I think.'

213

There was silence for a second then the ping of ricocheting bullets started up on the landing where the voice came from, followed by the clatter of empty casings landing on concrete above the staircase again. This was followed by a string of curses, then firing started up from the other end of the baths. Only this time it wasn't silenced and the noise echoing off the old concrete walls almost sounded like another bomb going off.

'Well, I don't know who they are,' said The Gecko, 'but they don't pay my rent, and I've got a train to catch.'

The major crossed his arms beneath his Thomas Cook vest and pulled out the two hand grenades. With a toss of his thumbs, he flicked the pins out and stood up, as whoever it was on both landings started blazing away at each other again, like the siege at Glenrowan. The Gecko tossed the first hand grenade underarm with his right hand up to the closest landing, then bowled the other one overarm onto the far landing. There was another burst of gunfire and the spray of bullets, then two simultaneous explosions followed by four simultaneous screams of pain. Les heard what sounded like the splash of a body landing in the pool and the thump of another one landing above their heads. The major stood up again; so did Les and Eddie. The body was on its back covered in blood and dust, but Les could still recognise the grey hair and the thick, jowly face lolled towards them.

'It's Boris. What the fuck's he doing here?'

'I don't think he was down here fishing, Les,' said the major.

'If he was, he sure picked a bad night.'

Eddie looked at them as if they were both talking Chinese. 'Well, I think that's that. Why don't we grab these bodies and get the shithouse out of here?'

In the crisp silence after all the gunfire and explosions, Les could hear the breeze outside the handball court and the waves swirling over the rocks below. He also could almost feel the awful moaning, creaking sound he'd heard earlier, it was getting that loud now. Les was going to remark on this and changed his mind.

'Yeah, good idea,' he nodded.

'They're just over here,' said the major.

Les padded over in the dust as the major pulled out a knife then knelt down and started digging away at the edge of the hump he'd been scuffing at earlier. Eddie put his gun away, got a knife out and did the same. In no time there was a small cloud of dust around them and they had the first body prised out. It was wrapped in an old, dry oilskin — dusty, grimy, smelly and plain horrible, in general. Disgusted, but surprised at how light it was, Les grabbed the oilskin and laid it on the ground alongside him. Eddie and the major started digging furiously again and, before long, had the second body out. Les took it and laid it down next to the other one.

'Right! That's it,' said Eddie, jumping out of the shallow hole they'd just dug. 'Let's piss off!'

The major didn't move. 'Hey, hang on, Eddie,' he said. 'There's another body down here.'

'There's what!?'

Eddie and Les peered into the hole where the major

215

had his torch flashing over something shining a dull, ash-coated black at his feet.

'That's a body bag, Eddie. You don't need me to tell you that.' The Gecko moved the beam up to Eddie's face. 'You never mentioned anything about this either.'

Eddie stared down at the body bag in total disbelief. 'Shit! It's not bloody mine. Shit! Well, throw it in with the others, but I'm fucked if I know where it came from, Garrick.'

'So you tell me.'

Eddie jumped back in the hole and helped Garrick dig the body bag out; Les bent down and took the end. It felt heavier than the two oilskins and even more horrible, and Les didn't like it one little bit. He didn't have a clue what was going on now. He was sure they were going to get sprung and all around him the dreadful, shuddering noise was getting louder like some crippled giant moaning out across the bay. Eddie and the major jumped out of the hole and picked up an oilskin each; Les took the body bag and the major's overnight bag. Then, like three dirty, filthy grave robbers in some Hammer movie, they clambered down the slope, half formed by the blast, to the rubber ducky rocking around gently nose-first where it was tied to the spike at the edge of the rockpool. Someone dressed in black, wearing a black balaclava, was standing in the front brandishing a paddle. Les didn't know the face, but he recognised the shape, and despite the horror show going on around him, he burst out laughing.

'Don't tell me. It's bloody Rambo, and he's joined the IRA.'

'Get fucked, Norton, you red-headed prick,' said

George Brennan. 'I need your smart-arse remarks like I need a hole in the fuckin' head. About six hundred rats as big as Dobermans just tried to jump in the boat.'

'Fuck the rats,' ordered Eddie, dumping his body in the back of the rubber ducky. 'Just get the motor started and let's get going.'

'Aye, aye, Captain.' George started moving to the back of the boat and hesitated. 'Shit! What's that noise?'

'Yes, I noticed it myself,' remarked the major. 'It appears to be getting louder.' He dropped his body in the back of the rubber ducky and climbed in alongside it.

Les dumped his body bag on top of the others and climbed in next to the major. 'I don't know what it is,' he said, wiping dust and sea spray from his face, 'but something definitely ain't right.'

'Just get the fuckin' boat going,' yelled Eddie, untying the line and turning the rubber ducky round so it faced the entrance to the rockpool. 'Well, come on, George, you fat cunt,' he said, jumping into the boat opposite Les and the major, 'what are you doing?'

George was belting away at the rope on the outboard motor trying to get it started, but, despite his curses and the frantic effort he was putting in, it refused to kick over. Les could hear sirens now and see lights coming on in all the surrounding blocks of units and other lights approaching the baths coming down Notts Avenue. The moaning, rumbling sound filling the air suddenly seemed to reach a horrible crescendo, then right before Norton's eyes the landing next to the stairs where the major threw the first hand grenade collapsed with a rumbling crash onto the landing below, sending great lumps of concrete and other debris smashing through the metal railing into the pool below. Seconds later, the railing alongside went and the entire front of the Icebergs Club came down with it, hurling more concrete, metal girders and bricks into the pool along with shattering panes of glass, flattened window panes and wrecked poker machines. Then the roof started to cave in and more sections of wall began tumbling down. The Gecko's low-yield nuclear device had blown out the handball court exactly as he planned, but the shockwaves had turned the concrete cancer rotting away through the rest of the place terminal and the entire old building was now in its death throes. Another wall collapsed along with more of the clubhouse and another row of windows, showering more shards of glass and debris across the pool. Everybody in the rubber ducky was watching in awe, including George, who was still trying frantically to start the motor, and Eddie, joining him with the cursing. Then the creaking noise seemed to hit this one dreadful note and the water in the pool started to bubble and churn. Fascinated at first, Les watched as a small crack appeared in the corner of the baths closest to them and water started to jet out like a firehouse. Next thing, the wall at that end seemed to quiver, then explode out from the weight of the water it had held back all those years. Norton's look of fascination soon turned to horror as a swirling wall of water about three metres high came racing towards them, along with the splintered wood, smashed glass and tonnes of other debris tumbling around inside it.

'George,' he shouted, 'get that motor going for Christ's sake, or we're rat shit.'

Just as Les called out, the motor kicked in. George gave it a quick rev, then gunned the rubber ducky straight out the entrance to the rockpool as the wave from the baths engulfed it. The rubber ducky hit the edge of the wave and flipped up into the air at an angle, almost turning over. Somehow it managed to straighten itself up, then slam back down on the other side with a thump that nearly sent the four of them sailing out of the boat along with the three bodies. George settled back down, gunned the motor again, then hung a sharp right and they headed straight out of Bondi Bay.

'Holy bloody shit!' yelled Eddie, above the roar of the outboard motor. 'How about that?' The little hit-man's adrenalin was still racing, and he could hardly keep to himself now he knew they were in the clear.

Norton was feeling pretty much the same. 'Jesus! I thought we were gone for a minute there. And we would have, too, if it hadn't have been for Rambo here.' George didn't reply but, hunched over the outboard motor, his eyes were still sticking out from under his balaclava like two boiled eggs.

'I've got a feeling I may possibly have used a drop too much red mercury,' said the major.

Norton made a gesture with one hand. 'Well, you can't say I didn't offer to help you, Major.'

Fading behind them in the wind and the foaming wake from the rubber ducky, the old Bondi baths was still subsiding bit by bit and there were several small fires now, caused by broken power lines sending showers of sparks into the smoking rubble. The entire sea wall of the baths had disintegrated and the main body of water was gone, but water was still pouring out, flushing whatever debris was left on the bottom of the pool with it. And floating or lying around somewhere were four bodies, along with their weapons.

'Well, you did it, Major,' said Eddie. 'Great job. You too, Les.' Eddie reached over and slapped the pair of them on the shoulder. 'I'll tell you what, Garrick, you should have seen the explosion from out here. It looked unbelievable. You sure know what you're doing.'

'Thank you, Eddie,' acknowledged the major, 'but there is one thing I'd like to discuss with you. I don't think you've been entirely honest with me, my boy.'

'Honest?' Eddie seemed genuinely hurt. 'What are you talking about, Major?'

The Gecko nodded to the ghastly pile sitting on the floor of the boat. 'The body bag, Eddie. There was nothing in the contract about a third body. Two, I was told.'

'Shit! I forgot all about the bloody thing.'

'Yes, so I'd noticed,' replied the major.

Eddie was adamant almost to the point of remorse. 'Mate, I swear, I don't know anything about it, or how it got there. Or who's in it. I know who's in the oil-skins, but I'm fucked if I know who or what's in the body bag.'

'Ohh yeah.'

While the wind flicked at their hair, Eddie and the major got into a mildly heated discussion about the body bag; with Eddie swearing on a stack of bibles Evel Knievel couldn't have jumped over that he knew nothing about it or who the blokes were shooting at

220

them from up on the landing. Sitting on the sidelines, Les could see that Eddie was telling the truth. Les also got the impression the major was winding Eddie up a bit as well. Finally the major appeared to accept Eddie's story.

'All right,' he conceded, 'I'll believe you this time, but don't let it happen again.'

Eddie grinned and pulled out his knife again. 'I suppose we should have a look and see what's in the bloody thing while we're here.'

'Ohh, Christ, Eddie,' said Les. 'Do you have to?'

'Yeah, why not? It might be full of money. It might be Elvis Presley.'

'Actually, I'm a little curious myself,' said the major.

The Gecko shone his torch over the body bag while Eddie went to stab his knife in the top and slash it open. He didn't need to. The thick plastic zipper still worked and Eddie was able to open it easily. Les stared into the torch's beam for a reluctant look. It was the skeleton of a man in an old blue tracksuit. Strips of dried brown skin clung to the bones, a thick mop of grey hair, now more a greasy brown, sat on the skull and whoever it was had a strong jawline. The eyes were just empty dried-out sockets with more skin spread tightly around them like brown Glad Wrap. A sickening gassy odour came from the bag — and how long the body had been in there was anybody's guess. Whatever. It definitely wasn't the nicest thing Les had ever seen, or smelled.

'Well, there's fuck all in here,' said Eddie. 'And it definitely ain't Elvis. This bloke's got a good head of hair. But no sideburns, baby.'

221

'Whoever it is,' said the major, 'he had a bloody good set of teeth. Have a look.'

'Yeah, you're right,' agreed Eddie. 'They're perfect.' He turned to Norton. 'Who do you reckon it is, Les? We know it's not Elvis.'

'I don't know and I don't care. Zip the fuckin' thing back up. It's giving me the creeps.'

'Heh-heh-heh!' Eddie went to zip the body bag back up and stopped. 'Hey, wait a minute. There is something in here.' Les thought he noticed the major's torch catch on a piece of plastic. Eddie pulled it out. It was a white T-shirt wrapped in a plastic bag sealed with durex tape and looked as good as the day it was put inside.

The Gecko ran his torch over it. On the left chest, printed in small blue letters, was the word THARUNKA.

'Tharunka', said the major. 'I'm just trying to think what that is.'

'Wasn't that something to do with a university back during the Vietnam War?' said Eddie. 'I can't remember for sure.' He gave the T-shirt another once-over and handed it to Norton. 'Here, Les, you have it. You like collecting T-shirts.'

'I don't want the fuckin' thing.'

'Go on, take it. It looks like your size.'

'Oh, all right.' Les took the T-shirt and stuffed it inside his vest, knowing Eddie was winding him up a bit and he could dump the grisly thing somewhere later.

They skimmed across the ocean another two kilometres or so until Bondi and the Eastern suburbs were just a spider web of light in the distance. Around them

was nothing but a breeze on their faces and inky black-
ness, punctuated occasionally by the moon appearing
briefly behind the clouds.

'How much further, Eddie?' asked Les.

Eddie looked at his watch. 'We're there.'

George slowed the rubber ducky down, the major
stood up and gave a couple of quick blips with his
torch and the aft lights on a game fishing boat lit up
about fifty metres away. George eased the rubber
ducky towards a metal ramp just above the propeller
and Les could see the name — *Splashdown*. He had
half an idea who owned it, when a voice with a kind of
wheezy chuckle in it boomed out, 'God strike me! It's
McHale's Navy and Rambo's the skipper. Stop the
fight, I'm getting out of here.'

The voice belonged to James D. Gloves, a happy-
go-lucky, dinky-di Aussie bloke who ran a fishing
magazine and did a show on radio. Gloves's three
loves in life were fishing, women and corny jokes
saturated with Australian rhyming slang. He was
holding a line above the metal ramp, and was wearing
jeans, a fishing cap and a fishing jacket over a dark
T-shirt.

'How are you, JD?' said Eddie. 'All right?'

'Horny as a Kimberleys cattle drive. You haven't got
a couple of Barossa Pearls in those bags, have you,
Eddie? I've got a larrikin's hat that hard you could
smash beer bottles on it. I'll give her one before they
go swimming. I don't mind a bit of necrophilia. An eye
for an eye and a stiff for a stiff. That's my motto.'

'No, no sheilas, JD,' said Eddie, 'just three blokes.
And I think their juices might be a bit dried up by now.'

'Oh, pooh!' said Gloves. 'Count me salmon and trout with the donut punching. I'll leave that for the horses' hoofs, thanks.'

Then a familiar voice came from behind Gloves. 'You blokes haven't got a set of industrial headphones in the boat, have you? Two hours trapped with this prick and I've got corns on my ears. He'd talk under ten feet of quicksand.'

'Shut up, Price, you whingeing bastard,' chuckled Gloves. 'You've never had so much fun in your life.'

Price ignored Gloves as he threw the line to Eddie and moved to the back of the fishing boat. 'Hello, Eddie,' he said. 'Hello, Les. Hello, Garrick. How are you? Everything go okay?'

'Everything went according to plan, Price,' replied the major. 'There might have been some slight structural damage to the baths, but that couldn't be avoided.'

'Don't worry about it,' said Price. 'How's thing's with you, Eddie? Everything all right?'

'Good as gold.'

'And you, Les. You okay too?'

'Yeah,' answered Norton. 'It's been . . . just wonderful.'

'Good on you, mate. We'll talk about it through the week.'

'Come on, let's get rid of these bodies,' said Eddie. 'Garrick's got a train to catch.'

'That's right,' said the major.

George and Eddie climbed onto the fishing boat and Les and the major began passing the bodies over. Gloves took them and lay them down on the deck next to a pile of old car batteries, gearboxes, chains and rope. Price was just as curious as the others about the third body, but Eddie said he'd discuss it with him later on. George stayed on the *Splashdown* and Eddie got back in the rubber ducky. He'd take Les and the major back to the boatsheds, leave it there, and drive home in his own car. Then they all said their quick goodbyes. Gloves hit the motor on *Splashdown* and the big fishing boat burbled out to sea. Eddie got the motor on the rubber ducky going with one pull, spun it around, and zapped back towards Bondi Bay. From there, they just skimmed across the ocean in silence, except for the howl of the outboard and the bump and slap as the rubber ducky would hit a small wave. The wind had dried the sweat off around Norton's neck, but it was quite cool, making him almost sneeze a couple of times and he hoped he wasn't getting a cold. Eddie gunned the rubber ducky and they were approaching Bondi Bay in what seemed like minutes. Eddie went straight in the middle, slowed down about halfway and turned the boat right towards the boatsheds at the north end.

People had started to gather on Ben Buckler Point and there were fire engines, police cars, TV trucks and crowds of people swarming around the south end of Bondi, gaping at the gutted remains of Bondi baths, when they cruised quietly up to the ramp at the bottom of the boatsheds. Eddie gunned the boat up on a small swell, cut the motor and jumped out the front. The major climbed out the front after him. Norton jumped out over the left side straight onto a slimy weed-covered rock and went arse over head, straight back into the water.

'Ahh, fuck!' cursed Les, as he clambered back on his feet, soaked to the skin.

'Fair dinkum,' said Eddie, 'fancy bringing you along. You boofhead great wombat.'

Even the major had to laugh.

'Ahh, fuck it!' Norton cursed again.

They ran the rubber ducky up the ramp next to the other boats. Eddie told them to piss off, they were running late for the major's train. He'd remove the outboard motor and leave it in a 44-gallon drum of water in one of the boatsheds, then let the rubber ducky down. If anyone did happen to come snooping around they'd find nothing; especially not a warm motor.

'Okay, Eddie.' The major gave him a quick handshake. 'I'll see you when you come up on Wednesday. Well done, lad.'

'Yes, sir. Well done.' Eddie snapped the major a salute and got one back. He turned to Norton as he started unbolting the outboard. 'I'll ring you tomorrow, Les.'

'Okay, Eddie. I'll see you then.' Les started up the stairs after the major.

'Oh, and Les.'

Norton turned around.

'Thanks, mate.'

'Yeah, no worries, Eddie.'

Les had given the major the keys and, by the time Les had squelched up to the car, the major had cleaned most of the dust from his face and clothes with his T-shirt and changed into a clean grey sweatshirt he'd had in the blue canvas bag. Les would have liked to have gone home and done the same thing, but the major had a train to catch. Les returned the major's bags to the back of the ute, got behind the wheel and, with his wet clothes soaking into the seat covers, headed straight towards Rose Bay, to avoid any traffic and sightseers and took a left at New South Head Road.

Not much was said on the trip to Central railway. The Gecko had gone all pensive and thoughtful or something, as if he was trying to put two and two together and it wasn't quite coming up the square root of sixteen. Norton, besides having a medium-range case of the shits, was just glad the thing was all over. And he never wanted to see another cup of coffee either. The major was a novelty and a bit of fun at first, but now Les would be glad to see the arse end of him. He just hoped the headlines in the morning paper would read MUSLIM EXTREMISTS DESTROY FAMOUS BONDI LANDMARK and that would be it. Bad luck about the four bodies they left behind.

They went past Edgecliff Station and approached the rise towards the Kings Cross tunnel. Yes, it had been a weird one, all right, mused Les. Who were those four blokes? He knew one was Boris. But what was he doing down there and why were they shooting at them? Probably, it was like the major had said and they'd blundered into a big drug deal or something. Surely they weren't after the other body? No, no way. Norton laughed mirthlessly to himself. Maybe they were. Maybe that was the FBI. There was an Australian connection there. The FBI hated Australians. Especially J. Edgar Hoover. He despised them. All because of an Australian called Harry

Bridges who was boss of the US West Coast Longshoremen's Union, and of what Harry Bridges did to the FBI at the Piccadilly Hotel in New York. He made them all look like dills. That could have been Jimmy Hoffa in the bag. He was a mate of Harry Bridges'. You didn't know that on your whiz-bang internet, Mark Prior, did you? You computer genius. Yeah, but my old man did. What a story, mused Les. What a night. What a dirty, stinken, rotten, low, forget-able bloody shitfight.

Next thing, they'd pulled up in almost the same place Les had parked when he picked the major up on Wednesday. Norton took the major's heaviest bag and squelched up alongside him to the Country Trains plat-form. Most of the water in Norton's clothes had soaked into the front seat of the car, but he was still awfully wet; especially his boots. They were still full of water and every now and again it would ooze through the lace holes or over the top and he'd leave a trail of soggy footprints. Plus all the fine dust, ash and grit from the explosion had been soaked or ground into him and Les was convinced there were some nuked cockroaches hidden on him somewhere. Norton had definitely seen better nights, but passengers and staff were very thin on the ground, so at least no one was staring at him when they walked up to the platform entrance where the major's train was leaving in about five minutes.

'Well, Les, what can I say?' he smiled.

'I don't really know, Major,' answered Norton, plac-ing the major's bag at his feet. 'But I've never been in, or seen anything like it before. Let me know the next time you're in Sydney, and I'll move to Perth.'

'Fair enough. I think I can understand, lad. But, none the less, I would like to shake your hand once more before I leave.'

'Yeah, why not,' agreed Les, 'even though on page 88 of the Jack Gibson bible, Ken Loefler says, "Most of the trouble in the world today is due to the handshake without meaning". I reckon this one's got some sort of meaning, Garrick.'

'An admirable quote, Les. You're obviously a man of good taste and intelligence.' They shook hands for the last time and the major went to pick up his bag. 'Oh, before you go, Les, do you mind if I have another look at that T-shirt? You didn't lose it when you went on your tit, did you?'

'No, it's still here.' Les took the T-shirt from inside his vest and handed it to the major. Apart from a few smears of water across the plastic bag it was still in brand-new condition.

The major looked at the printing on the front. 'Tharunka,' he said quietly. 'That definitely was one of the university students' papers I saw out during the Vietnam War. Do you mind if I open it. Les? I think there's something printed across the back.'

Les shrugged an indifferent reply and the major pulled the T-shirt from its plastic bag and held it up. Printed across the back in blue lettering was WATCH YOUR FISH AND CHIPS. THE PRIME MINISTER IS MISSING.

Norton looked at it just as indifferently. 'What sort of a clown would put a T-shirt like that in a body bag?'

'Yes, what sort of a clown indeed?' nodded the major slowly. 'Someone with a sense of humour, wouldn't you say? A bit of a joker, Les?'

229

'Yeah,' grunted Norton. 'A regular Rodney bloody Rude.'

'Les?' asked the major. 'Do you particularly want this T-shirt?'

'Not really. I've got heaps of the bloody things.'

'Okay if I have it?'

'It's all yours, Garrick.'

'Thanks, Les.' A whistle blew and the major picked up his bag. 'That's my train. I'll be in touch.'

'All right, Major. I'll see you again some time.'

The Gecko ran for his train. Les turned and squelched his way back out to the car; only with a limp this time. He didn't tell anyone, but when he fell out of the rubber ducky he'd torn his arse on barnacles. The cuts hurt like buggery now and they'd hurt a lot more when he put iodine on them back at the flat. Plus it looked like he *was* getting a cold. Norton let out two horrible sneezes and spat on the ground. Yes, he was getting a cold all right. He wiped his fingers under his nose and flung that on the ground as well. Jokers with a sense of humour, Les snorted, as he opened the car door and climbed onto the soaking wet front seat. If there was anything funny about tonight, you can root me.